MY COUSIN
KILLED HITLER

MY COUSIN KILLED HITLER

Zhukov's Shocking Secret of World War II Revealed

Hera Jaclyn Becker, M.B.A.

MY COUSIN KILLED HITLER
ZHUKOV'S SHOCKING SECRET OF WORLD WAR II REVEALED

iUniverse books may be ordered through booksellers or by contacting:

iUniverse
1663 Liberty Drive
Bloomington, IN 47403
www.iuniverse.com
844-349-9409

Because of the dynamic nature of the Internet, any web addresses or links contained in this book may have changed since publication and may no longer be valid. The views expressed in this work are solely those of the author and do not necessarily reflect the views of the publisher, and the publisher hereby disclaims any responsibility for them.

Any people depicted in stock imagery provided by Getty Images are models, and such images are being used for illustrative purposes only.
Certain stock imagery © Getty Images.

Please visit the author's website at http://www.happyfatheringday.com

ISBN: 978-1-4502-2191-7 (sc)
ISBN: 978-1-4502-2192-4 (hc)
ISBN: 978-1-4502-2193-1 (e)

Library of Congress Control Number: 2010905430

Print information available on the last page.

iUniverse rev. date: 11/29/2023

This book is dedicated to my great-grandfather Isak "Jak", who in his devotion to and protection of his first cousin Marshal Georgi Zhukov, managed to keep the secret.

I also dedicate this book to my cousin Marshal Zhukov himself. It is my hope that he will now receive the respect and recognition he has so long been deserving of from the entire world, and that all children's World History textbooks will contain a significant portion dedicated to him and to his accomplishments that serve as probably the greatest lesson in tolerance the world has ever known.

As Marshal Georgi Zhukov himself dedicated his own memoirs to his men who served so valiantly under his leadership, I dedicate this book to them as well. It is with my deepest gratitude that I also dedicate this book to all the very brave and self-sacrificing service men and woman of all nations and to their families. May all people never again know the suffering caused by World War II, because of one man, Hitler, and his contagious, discriminatory, and evil agenda.

PREFACE

our quotes pertain to *My Cousin Killed Hitler* and they are:

"In Europe the war has been won and to no one man do the United Nations owe a greater debt than to Marshal Georgi Zhukov (for the defeat of Nazi Fascism and termination of the Holocaust)."

-General Dwight D. Eisenhower June 1945
Supreme Commander-Allied Expeditionary Force

"The Party may succeed in keeping Zhukov's figure out of the public eye but it will not succeed in keeping his memory out of the hearts of men."

-Krishna Menon, 1957
Indian Ambassador to Moscow

How many students, to whom World War II is now musty history, recognize at once the name of Georgi Zhukov?.....How many are aware that this is the man, best described by Harrision E. Salisbury, who "will stand above all others as the master of the art of mass warfare in the twentieth century?"

-Martin Caidin, *The Tigers Are Burning*

"In fact, Hitler's Germany was defeated, first and foremost, by the Soviet Union, (under Marshal Zhukov's leadership and by his ingenious military strategies). Some 70-80 percent of German combat forces were destroyed by the Soviet military on the Eastern front. The D-Day landing in France by American and British forces, which is often portrayed in the United States as a critically important military blow against Nazi Germany, was launched in June 1944 -- that is, less than a year before the end of the war in Europe, and months after the great Soviet military victories at Stalingrad and Kursk, which were decisive in Germany's defeat."

-Mark Weber, *The "Good War" Myth of World War II*

World War II is a difficult subject to write about knowing all the suffering and loss that people of the world have endured because of one mad man and his obsession with ruling the world. I personally know the pain of this grief, as one relative of mine was killed in Po Valley, Italy, in the spring of 1945. He was on ski patrol when the Nazis opened fire on his men. He valiantly stood up and took the fire, helping some of his men escape. He was awarded the Silver Star posthumously. I visit him at the cemetery and also mourn for his dear father, who from the grief of losing his only son, drank himself into an early grave.

My Cousin Killed Hitler was written for three purposes. One purpose was to accurately convey the point that it was Marshal Georgi Zhukov, my fourth cousin, who directly led to Hitler killing himself and Hitler ordering his own body burned. Hitler did this because Marshal Zhukov was only about one hundred meters away from him in Berlin in the spring of 1945, and he knew Zhukov would drag his dead body throughout the streets of Moscow. It was not just a collection of Generals and soldiers both for the Soviets and the Allies who ended Hitler, as many of us have been told or have been taught in school, but rather it was the ingenious military leadership of Marshal Zhukov of the Soviet Union. I greatly respect all the efforts and valiant service of the military men and women in World War II, including those in D-Day, and think about them frequently with deepest gratitude; however, it was the leader Marshal Zhukov without whom it would not have all come together to result in the end of Hitler. In this way, the people of the world will clearly know to whom they owe their freedom from the tyranny of Nazi rule. People will also know that it was Zhukov who was the first to liberate a concentration camp, which was Majdanek, in July 1944. In addition, he was the man who ordered his soldiers from the Red Army to liberate Auschwitz. Through his military genius in the defeat of Hitler, Zhukov brought an end to the Holocaust.

The second purpose for writing *My Cousin Killed Hitler* was to negate the censorship of this man who was second in command of the Soviet Union during World War II and who saved the world from Hitler's rule. This censorship had been ongoing for many years. One way this should be done is by encouraging those in administrative positions, who oversee historical entities throughout the world, to advocate that Marshal Zhukov be given plaques, statues, or permanent exhibits, etc., which will serve to educate the public as to their indebtedness to this great man. Another way this should be done is for high school teachers to consider encouraging or requiring their students to read *My Cousin Killed Hitler*.

The third purpose was to inform all people about the great, shocking secret of World War II, which was held by Marshal Zhukov for over sixty-years, and by my great-grandfather, who was Zhukov's first cousin. The secret has just recently been uncovered by this author, who felt it an undeniable obligation to bring to the world. It is a secret that will serve as one of the greatest, if not the greatest, lesson in tolerance all people will ever know, and it will serve a utilitarian usefulness to see that tolerance becomes more of a standard practice in life for all.

My Cousin Killed Hitler is based on true, accurate, historical events and dates, along with my proprietary family knowledge of Georgi Zhukov from birth through much of his life that include the memoirs which really do exist and for which the KGB tried to prevent from getting out to the world. It includes the addition of an intriguing and interesting storyline that depicts Zhukov's fictional daughter experiencing the harrowing efforts she incurred to see that his memoirs get out to the world, while she herself learns of all her papa's victories, frustrations, and personal secret. The ultimate goal of this story was to both educate and entertain while serving to see that all people will now know the truth about WWII.

The book opens in the year 1974. The General Council of the Soviet Party has received word that Marshal Zhukov is on his deathbed. The Council is concerned that its effort to write its own version of Soviet history, which inaccurately depicted many of its members as great heroes, will be deemed self-serving. Now that Zhukov is dying, the Council decides to act upon undercover information which reported that Zhukov had written a second but true account of the historical events he was personally involved with through his memoir contained in a journal.

With its determination to keep each individual member's aggrandized role in Soviet history intact, the Council sends three secret police officers out to retrieve the journal and destroy it. However, the determination of a fallen hero should never be underestimated. Zhukov, a man who lives by the truth, knows his life is coming to an end. In an effort to pass the truth on to posterity, he gives his beloved daughter the dangerous mission of getting his journal, which contains his memoir, out to the world...

THE START OF THE PRESENT DAY JOURNEY

I am running from a pack of wolves, or at least they seem like a pack of wolves to me. I am merely a twenty year old girl who has led a reclusive life. Yet, these men dressed in the dark blue uniforms of the Soviet secret police are relentless in tracking me down. Constantly, I turn around to see if they have closed in on me as my legs propel me forward. Are they going to take on the persona of a thunderstorm of dark blue color uniforms? Are they going to roll up behind me, the sounds of their footsteps like the thunder rumbling in the distance? Are they going to take on their wolf-like persona and attack me with their sharp fangs digging deep into my flesh until the warm blood that runs through my veins drains out of me? The manner, in which my pursuers may ambush me, causes me anxiety.

I continue to run through the sea of cement that makes up the streets. Every time I hear something behind me, my stride grows longer and my pace quickens. People on the streets stop what they are doing to watch me, probably thinking I am an insane person or maybe even a thief who is stealing this journal I am holding tightly in my arms. Oh, this heavy journal is the bane of my existence and the reason I am running for my life.

Just as I turn the corner, my foot catches an uneven part of the street. CRUNCH! The horrible crunching sound comes from my big toe as the journal is loosened from my arms and flies through the air until it lands a couple of feet in front of where I have fallen to the ground. Excruciating pain is shooting through my leg, from my big toe. I probably broke it. The pain from my scraped and bruised knee adds to my agony. The sharp pains permeate throughout my whole body. My feet are throbbing from all the running. My hands are burning at the spots where I land with my whole weight, and my head is pulsating from the overwhelming sensations. I try hard to catch my breath, but my lungs feel like they are on fire from the intense running I have been doing.

Slowly, I lift my head to see where the journal has landed. It has landed with the pages face down and is open so the front and back covers are looking up at me. I study the beautiful letters on the cover with the title, "The Truthful Memoirs" by Marshal Georgi Zhukov. My eyes scan back and forth over the words "Marshal Georgi Zhukov". My mind wanders back to the events of that morning, before my life became chaotic and in complete turmoil…

Earlier this morning while following my mundane routine, I woke up early to prepare breakfast for my Papa and myself and do the many other chores I had. I took my role as woman of the house very seriously. Actually, it was more appropriate to be known as woman of the apartment. Our apartment was very small, containing just three rooms. When you walked in through the front door, to the right was the kitchen. The only things contained in the kitchen were a stove, icebox, small sink, and a table with chairs. Walking out of the kitchen and past the front door, you reached my papa's office/bedroom. His office contained a desk that faced the window and bookshelves with numerous volumes of novels within them. My papa enjoyed reading his books. Every once in a while, I would grab a book off the shelf and delve into its yellowed pages. Most of my papa's books were very old. Before I would choose a book to read, I would admire the bindings of the book, which showed their age. My papa had most of these books for many years. I never recalled him getting any newer novels, as if he was cut off from the world and had to be satisfied with what he had in his collection. This room appeared like an office at first glance, and the only way you could tell it took on the characteristics of a bedroom was by the small bed in the corner of the room which my papa slept on. This room is where he spent most of his time.

My time was spent down the short hallway from my papa's office/bedroom. My room was located on the opposite side of the hallway and was about half the size of my papa's. It looked like it was a closet that was converted into a small living quarter for me to reside in. My bed was in the corner, and I had a small table on the opposite side. It was cramped, but I didn't mind too much. I was always up and roaming about, completing some kind of chore.

As I stated before, I was now the woman in the household. My mother died giving birth to me, so I never really had a childhood. My earliest memory was doing chores, although that memory was a distant one to me. I went to school for a short while, but then decided to study at home under my papa's tutelage. Even at a young age, I felt very different from the other children. In some way, I managed to befriend one girl with whom I remained friendly for a long time. Yes, my dear friend Sasha was more like a sister to me. I had a much older sister, but I was never very close with her. She had already been married with children of her own when I was born. Sasha took the place of my absent sister for me, so I wouldn't feel the pain of being ignored by a sibling who wanted nothing to do with me.

I carefully placed the water on the stove to boil for my papa's tea. My papa enjoyed drinking his tea every morning and evening, without fail. My darling papa was everything to me. I knew he had become a prominent figure in the Soviet army, but it was unusual that we never lived a life of grandeur that one would expect. I knew he was something special and had done great things when he was in his position of power; I just never knew exactly what he did. He never talked to me about it. Whenever I asked, he would just stop and have that far away, sad look in his eyes. Trying to research his accomplishments proved futile. It was as if he never existed. So whenever someone stopped him to express their gratitude to him, I wondered exactly what he had done to deserve this. My papa would just smile and go on about his business like nothing ever happened. I remembered looking at him inquisitively, my eyes searching for an answer in his face and hoping my look would stir him to explain it to me. At these times, he would just look at me and shake his head no. The sadness in his eyes conveyed to me that he didn't want to divulge that part of his past. Out of respect for his unspoken wishes, I didn't pursue it any further.

My attention focused back on the task at hand and, I checked the water to make sure it was boiling. I proceeded to my papa's room, knocked on the door and slowly opened it. "Good morning, Papa. What would you like for breakfast today?" Instead of being in bed, he was at his desk, busily writing in his journal. "Papa, please lie down." I was concerned that he was working himself too hard.

"NO!" he turned and snapped at me. I was taken aback by this. My papa was normally so gentle with me. I don't think I was as shocked by his tone as I was by his face. My papa had been sick for a long time, barely surviving two heart attacks, but now he was alarmingly sickly looking. His face was so pale, it looked like he had died and had come back in the form of a specter. His eyes were trying so hard to focus on his task at hand and on me, but I knew they were looking towards that light everyone talks about seeing when they are headed to the other side. I knew death was trying to ensnare him into its open arms. My papa could feel this just as I could see what was happening before my very eyes.

"I'll make us some soup," I said. I couldn't focus on my thoughts after seeing my papa like this. He simply looked at me blankly and turned back around. He began to write furiously again, clearly fighting his waning energy with his waxing desire to finish whatever he was doing. He had been working on that writing for years. I had no idea what he was writing, but it was clearly something of the utmost importance to my papa.

I made my way out the door and back into the kitchen. An uneasy feeling came over me when I thought about how my papa looked. I carefully poured his tea from the kettle into his favorite mug. I watched the water pour out in slow motion. The hot steam gently blew into my face and provided me with a temporary reprieve from my worries. Outside, the weather was cold and the heater in our house was shoddy at best. The heat cascaded gently down my body, from my face through my torso and into my arms straight down through my legs.

I was completely consumed by this warmth and in a trance-like state when a loud crash brought me back down to earth. The sound scared me so much; I dropped the half full kettle which caused water to splatter everywhere. In what felt like slow motion to me, I darted towards my papa's room where the sound came from. The slow motion sensation caused my legs to feel heavy, perhaps from fear of what I might find upon entering the room. Perhaps I was having an out of body experience, completely dissociating myself from the present circumstance that something happened to my papa. My slow motion feeling finally caught up with me and all that excess energy was used to burst through my papa's bedroom door. Frantically, I looked to the desk where he was sitting, but he and the chair were gone. Down on the floor, I heard rustling.

"Tatyanna, help me," my papa moaned. I made my way over to the other side of the room. He was lying helplessly on the floor; the heavy chair was on top of him and prevented him from moving.

"Papa," I cried out. I worked tirelessly and with all my energy to get the heavy chair off of him. Slowly, I helped him up onto his bed. He sat on the edge for a moment, shaking and struggling to catch his breath. I touched his arm and then gently laid him down. I sat on the bed beside him, gently caressing his arm. It was frightening how well his pale complexion blended perfectly with the white pillow, almost to the point where you could only tell it was his face from his eyes, nose, and mouth peeping out. He writhed in pain as he was groaning loudly. His eerie groaning sounded like a call to welcome death. Tears slowly started streaming down my face watching my papa in such horrible pain.

"Taty, please…get me the…" he said slowly while he pointed down at the ground to the red journal.

I slowly bent down and looked up at him, while holding his journal and asked," This, papa?"

He nodded, but it was more like he just bobbed his head slowly up and down. I sat back up on the bed and carefully examined the journal. What was this thing that consumed much of my papa's life? What was so important about it that my papa seemed to stall death's impending grasp to finish it? My papa appeared to have read my mind as he responded with answers to my questions.

"That journal…you have in your hands…is going to correct all…" he struggled to get his words out. The battle continued between my papa's will to survive in order to tell me about this and death's stronghold over him.

"Papa, what are you talking about?"

He closed his eyes, inhaled a large gulp of air, and held it in for a few moments as he tried to relax in a meditative state. In those short few moments, he fought the battle against death within himself. He opened his eyes slowly, and the look in them showed he had won this battle and had temporarily held off death's firm grasp. His eyes had life in them again and he had an energy that had been absent in him for a long time. Finally, taking a deep breath, he looked over at me. "That journal is going to tell what really happened. That ungrateful Stalin tried to keep me hidden and threw me away like a useless old shoe. And all the hurtful lies they made up about me!" My papa's deep seeded anger beamed through his eyes as he furrowed his brow.

"Relax papa. You're going to make yourself worse."

He turned to me and slowly lifted his arm up towards me. Gently stroking my face, he looked at me with great love in his eyes, the way a proud papa would look at his daughter. A twinkle sparkled in his eye as he stroked my face. "I love you so much, my little princess."

I smiled at him even though I was fighting back tears. I knew this would be the last time I would share a special moment with my papa ever again. "I love you too, papa."

"I know you love me, and that is why it hurts me to put this incredible burden on your shoulders."

I looked at him inquisitively, but before I could question him, he started moaning in pain once again. His temporary victory against death was short lived as its grasp began to take hold once again. He dropped his hand from my face and gripped at his chest while he writhed in immense pain. "You have to...get this journal out...for the world to see," he tried desperately to tell me through the pain, "my memoir...my story."

I looked back down at the journal, opened it, and flipped through the pages. My papa, even in his weak state, managed to snatch the journal from my hands. "Why did you do that?"

"You need...to listen to me very...carefully. They are coming for...this. You have to get...out of here. Find a safe hiding...place to read."

"Who is coming here? What have you been writing in here that's so important, papa? Please tell me!"

"The secret police...you are in great...danger. Leave now. They know...my end is..."

"The secret police put me in danger? How could you make me do something like this when I need to be with you right now?"

"Don't argue...with me. I'm asking you...please do this...for me. Just leave me...I'll be fine."

Just then, a car came to a screeching halt on its brakes right outside. Startled, I jumped up and looked out the window. Three men dressed in the dark blue uniform of the Soviet secret police hurriedly made their way out of a dusty black car. They were all tall men and you could see their bulging muscles through their uniforms. Their guns were resting ominously in their holsters as they marched up to our front door. BOOM! BOOM! BOOM! The way they pounded on our door made their presence known and was unlike someone who wanted to be invited kindly into your home. No, the way they banged on the door wasn't an invitation to be friendly. They hit the door with such force, trying to break it down with their fists.

I don't know if he was trying to stir me to act or just attempting a last stand against these threatening men, but it worked in galvanizing me into action. With the footsteps getting closer, I grabbed the journal. Before I made my way over to hide in the small crawl space under the floor, I quickly turned back around to my papa. "How could you do this to me?" I snapped in a whisper. Then, I quickly opened this hatch and hid inside.

"Where is it?" I could hear the man shouting at my papa. While in the dusty crawl space, I made my way down the hallway and looked quickly up through the separated slats in the floor of the room. I quickly tried to reason in my head where I should go. My head was sorting through all the possibilities of getting out to the open street. Opening a window would be a possibility, but they were always so hard to open. Even if it eventually would open easily, now was not the time to experiment. Should I try to escape out the back door? No, that would be a bad choice as it made a horrible creaking sound, and sometimes got stuck on the hinge when it was barely opened. What should I do? I came to the conclusion that there was only one way out of the apartment and that was through the front door. But I would have to get past the open doorway of my papa's room where the predators were in order to get out. Should I risk it, even with holding my papa's important journal in my arms? Do I dare tempt the fate of being caught and killed and risk my papa's story being lost forever? I started to creep slowly out of the hatch and gently placed my foot down. I closed my eyes and bit hard on my lower lip, fearful the floor would make a loud creaking noise. When no sound resonated from the floor, I put my other foot down gently and held my breath. No sound again. I placed my feet one in front of the other at a swifter pace down the hall until right before reaching the opening of the front door. The problem was my papa's room was the last one and it looked straight out into the hallway towards the front door. I had to figure out a way that I could make it safely out of the front door without the wolves seeing me. Peeking carefully into the room, the three of them were ravaging the place, ripping out the drawers from my papa's desk and dumping the contents contained inside onto the floor, and going into his closet and ripping things out. Even though they were busily chipping away at the room and making a raucous sound, my papa laid there perfectly still. His eyes were so peaceful, a kind of peace I can honestly say I had never seen before. That peace showed me he had left all the problems in this life behind and no one would ever bother him again. At that moment, even though I was still a bit upset about this enormous task my papa had given to me, I realized this was a part of his legacy which he left behind and trusted that I was strong enough to do this for him.

While they were still ravaging the room, I quickly darted past and down the last part of the hallway. I watched the opening where the front door had been pushed ajar, as it got closer and closer to me. I couldn't tell you how happy I was until…CREAK! The floorboard close to the door decided to betray me and let my enemies know my whereabouts. When I heard them stop their desperate search, I quickly ran towards the opening before they could get to me. "There she is!" one of the men shouted.

Instead of the front door opening widely for me and wishing me a safe journey by welcoming me through, it stopped right on its hinges with only a little sliver to squeeze through. I desperately tried pulling at the door to make it release its stubborn grasp, but to no avail. I had no other choice but to squeeze through the doorway. Even though I am thin, it was no easy task to do. Just before I went all the way through to the other side, my arm was tugged back with great force. The tug of war continued for a few moments, while one of the others tried unsuccessfully to pull open the door. With one final burst of energy, I got my arm free and heard a loud thud on the other side. Either he fell to the floor or the force caused him to plunge backwards and hit the wall.

I ran until I heard a loud stream of bullets. I watched in shock as the three of them had shot through the door and were now running outside past the gun smoke and dust from what was left of the tattered door.

Thoughts wildly ran through my head as I continued running. Just run. Don't look back. Keep picking up your legs higher and higher. Come on. Extend your stride. You can't let these predators get you...

That is how I got to this point of laying on the ground in complete nauseating pain. I try to bend my toe, but it will not bend. I'm bloody, bruised, and broken. Can anything else possibly go wrong on this very difficult day? Then, I hear a car race behind me and I turn around. There it is, the phantom black car carrying my predators. Perhaps they smell my blood, fear, and helplessness and that's how they have found the vicinity I am in. Fortunately, they soon pass me in the opposite direction.

Too close for comfort, I think to myself. So, I slowly pick myself up from the ground and dust my clothes off. I make my way over to pick up the journal and try to bend down. Pins and needles shoot through my knee and permeate throughout my leg. Somehow, I manage to pick up the journal. I continue on my way by hobbling, but tears are streaming down my face from the pain. I have to walk on the heel of my foot containing the broken toe and have to keep my knee as straight as possible to prevent the pain again. Where can I go? Where won't they find me? I look around the area I am in. I can see smaller houses in very poor condition surrounded by buildings housing storefronts. Who do I know that lives around here? Come on, Tatyanna, think.

Then, suddenly, it becomes clear to me. Sasha! Sasha lives close by. I find it very odd I had been thinking of her just this morning. Maybe placing thoughts of her in my head was God's way of trying to help me. I hobble along once again, as fast as I can. When I see that beautiful sight of her blue door staring me in the face, I smile through my tears. Trying to work my way up the few steps at her house is excruciating. Sasha must hear me inside because she quickly opens the door to see what is going on.

"Taty!" she shouts.

"Sasha, I need to ask you a favor," I plead with her, as I throw myself into the house and slam the door behind me.

"What happened to you? Why are you bleeding and dirty?"

She keeps questioning me and I am growing frustrated. I try to keep my patience with her, but how can I with three grown men who want a taste of my blood. "Look, Sasha, I don't have time right now to explain everything to you. To be honest, I don't even know why I'm in danger but I am. My papa died this morning…"

"Oh my God, Taty, I'm so sorry…"

"Please, let me finish," I snap. "He gave me this journal he's been working on for years to read. Can I stay here and hide to read this and see what all this is about?"

"Of course, you're always welcome here."

At that point, I am debating whether I should tell her who is pursuing me. Maybe if I keep it from her, she will not be in danger. Then again, if I don't tell her and something happens to her, I would feel unbearable guilt that I couldn't live with. "You could be in grave danger," I blurted out.

"What do you mean?" She looks confused.

"The police officers are after me. Well, actually they're after this journal, but since I'm the one currently in possession of it, I guess that means they are after me too. So, by me being in danger and you helping me, that means you're putting yourself at risk too."

She looks down at the journal in my arms. "What's in there?"

"Sasha, I don't know and I can't be out here talking about it." I burst further into the house and look around, trying to find a place to hide.

"Taty, go to the last room at the end of the hall on the left. It's my bedroom. You'll be safe in there."

I stand there and look at her for a moment. "Are you sure you still want to help me? I don't know what they're capable of doing," I say. I bite down on my lip, thinking of how the officers shot through my front door.

"Don't be ridiculous. Just go into my room and read. It was obviously important to your papa. You know he was like a second papa to me, and I would do anything to help him…and you."

I warmly hug her and run back into her room, quickly shutting the door. I go over and draw the blinds in her room so no one can peep in and see me. My eyes dart around the room. The room is fairly small. Her big bed is carefully set by the window. She has a single dresser on the opposite side of the room. It is a dark chocolate mahogany color, so beautiful and rich in detail. My papa had given it to her as a present some years ago. By the door is her closet that merely has a curtain over it, separating her room from the prying eyes of her belongings that were kept in there. I open the curtain. There are some clothes and shoes. Boxes are stuffed with various items, and they are piled up neatly around the perimeter of the floor. No, it's too cramped and not light enough to read, I think to myself. Finally, my eyes settle on the corner of the room by the bed. I really have no other choice. I can just dart under the bed if someone comes in here.

I limp over to the corner and sit down. Stretching out my legs and leaning my back up against the wall, I rest the journal on my lap. I brush my hand on the beautiful cover, with the rich leather and the gold letters shining brightly. Slowly, I pull the cover open and stare at the page. My papa had beautiful handwriting. I study the gentle cursive he wrote with and the winding curves of his letters. I close my eyes and take a slow, deep breath. Slowly, I exhale and open my eyes. Now I am ready for my job, and that is to be the protector and promulgator for the contents of my papa's journal, the contents I will now relay...

MY HUMBLE ROOTS

To really know me, Georgi Zhukov, is to know where I came from. I was born in 1896 in a poor village to parents who unfortunately were even poorer than the village's population. I say unfortunately not because of any shame I have, but because my parents were good people who deserved more. I have never been ashamed of where I came from. My humble beginnings helped mold me into the person I became and would be advantageous to me in the difficulties I faced in my career. Deep down, I know my papa was a good person and loved me, but he felt as patriarch of the household he had to be firm and give off a hardened exterior. That was always the impression he gave, but I think it was life's unfair hand that hardened him. He worked tediously in the fields to feed his family, but there was somehow barely enough food for my mother, younger sister, and myself. He was frustrated he couldn't provide more, but he never once complained.

I was always extremely close with my mother. She was much younger than my papa, but yet had the wisdom and sense of someone of equal age to my papa. She too worked hard in the fields. She would leave the house so early in the morning that it was dark outside and she wouldn't return until very late at night with matching darkness to her morning exit.

On one particular day when I was about fifteen, I was sitting on a chair and waiting for her. My papa and sister had gone out, so I was alone in our small house. I looked around at our house, if that's what you could call it. It was more like a one room shack. We had a single small table just enough for the four of us to sit around with four chairs. There were three cots around each bare wall. We were only able to get three cots, so I was forced to sleep on the floor. The few possessions I had in the world were neatly folded into a corner. Along the fourth wall, we had a counter that was completely bare. We kept it that way so we could keep our food there, but it was always empty. We lived day by day as far as food went and never had anything stored there long term. I just sat and stared out the window, hoping my mother would have some delicious food for us soon. My stomach violently grumbled. The vibration against the wall of my stomach reminded me just how empty my stomach really was.

I was fidgeting with the gold chain around my neck to ease my nerves and anxiety. It wasn't made of real gold, but it had been in my family for years. My mother gave it to me a few years back. My fingers gently caressed the crevices of the necklace, up and down, up and down. I closed my eyes to enjoy the tactile sensation that helped calm me.

A creak outside interrupted my pleasure. The door slowly opened and my mother appeared. Her face and clothes were covered in dirt. The clothes she wore were tattered, just like mine. The dejected look in her eyes cut through my soul. I hated when my mother looked like that. I knew that look meant she wasn't able to get any food for us. She stood there and looked at me. My stomach wanted to grumble so badly, but I tried every way I could to stop it. I squirmed in my chair and made rustling noises so the sound would be muffled for my mother's ears. I was no match for my violent hunger and my stomach wanted to let out a loud battle cry that it was going to win the war against me.

GRRRRRRRRRRRRRRRRRRR, that sound pushed my mother into worse despair. She put her face into her hands and started to sob violently. I jumped up from my chair and wrapped my arms around my mother. "Mama, please don't cry. We'll be fine."

"Don't patronize me, Georgi," she snapped at me.

I pulled back a little in shock. It was very uncharacteristic of her to snap. All the frustration and exhaustion she felt seemed to culminate into that outburst. I could understand it and knew I shouldn't take it personally. I stroked her back with gentle glides, caressing her like I caressed my necklace. "It'll be ok, mama."

"Don't you understand? No matter how hard I work, how long I work, all the extra effort I put in, I can't make enough. Never, never," she violently sobbed again until the door opening interrupted.

I looked up. My little sister was the first to walk through the door, followed by my papa. His graying hair was unkempt and his round face showed deep wrinkles from years of aggravation. He was a stout man with a wide build. Papa carried several loaves of bread in his arms. While he carefully placed all the loaves on our empty counter, my mother rapidly tried to wipe her eyes and her cheeks to clear any evidence that she had been crying. I know she didn't want my papa to see her breakdown.

My attention quickly turned back to the bread. The dark chocolate color of the bread made my mouth water. My eyes grew larger as they worked their way from top to bottom, taking in the beautiful sight of food. My nose breathed the warm delicious smell and my stomach started to grumble again. I started to fantasize about eating the bread, ripping a piece off and slowly putting it towards my anxiously awaiting mouth. When my tongue felt the hard warmth, it slowly closed so my teeth could dig into its crunchy exterior.

My little sister tugged gently at my shirt to get my attention. "Isn't it great, Georgi? All this food is so good!"

"Be quiet Oksana," my papa snapped while giving her a scolding look. She quickly let go of my shirt and dejectedly looked down at the floor.

I stroked her hair to try to comfort her and let her know it was alright. "Papa, where did you get all this from?"

"Mrs. Morislav. She was able to make more bread and offered us some, thanks to your sister's urging," he said sarcastically. My papa must have scolded her about asking Mrs. Morislav about the bread because after he said that her lip started to quiver like she was about to cry. She looked up at me, tears already started to fill her eyes. "I didn't want to take it, but she insisted." My papa's pride was hurt from accepting a handout, but I was so thankful we were going to have good bread for a while.

I wanted to get my sister out of this uncomfortable situation. "I'm going to take Oksana over to Mrs. Morislav. I personally want to thank her," I said. Before my papa could answer, I grabbed my sister's hand and we headed out the door. The night was very cool. The black sky blanketed the city and the stars twinkled brightly. My sister still looked down as she kicked the dirt from the road around.

"Oksana, don't worry about what Papa says. He just wants to be able to provide for his own family and not take food from other people. Most of us in the village are starving. He doesn't want to take anything from anyone." I stopped walking and bent down until I was looking up at her face. I gently stroked her cheek while tears were rolling down.

"I'm sorry. I didn't mean to be bad. I won't do it again. I promise."

"Don't be upset. You didn't do anything wrong, ok? You know I would tell you if it was wrong, but did you hear that come out of my mouth?" I cocked my eyebrow in a mischievously questioning way. Oksana shook her head no. "Then everything is ok," I said while tickling her. She had the most adorable laugh that could melt the thickest ice with its incredible warmth.

Our tender moment was interrupted by a sudden rumbling in the ground. The rumbling grew more fierce as a cacophony of the beating of horse hooves drew closer. I stood up and looked out over the horizon. A sea of horses was making their way towards us. Horses of all different colors- bay, chestnut, white, and black- were drawing closer and closer. There was a single horse leading the way. As it came closer, I could see a Commander of the Army sitting tall and proud on the horse. He was leading his men as they followed steadily behind him.

When the Commander saw me, he stopped directly in front of me. I recognized him immediately. Whenever I could, I would read books my neighbor managed to smuggle in for me. They were extremely hard to come by, but somehow she managed to get them. At night when my family was sound asleep, I would open the book and try to catch the light of the moon so I could see. One book I had read was about this particular Commander who stood before me whose name was Borzniov. The book contained a photograph of him, and he looked almost the same as in the picture but older. In the photo, he was decorated with all his medals as I now saw before me. The book made him out to be some great warrior, some hero. I heard the truth from my friends about what a monster he was, how he would beat and kill innocent civilians. He hated the Jews and would lead his men through towns where they resided and just burn down their houses. When those poor people would run in fear from their burning houses, he would just shoot them. I guess he was born into the façade of self importance. He came from a very wealthy family, and it was rumored he didn't perform well on his tests to get into the military school. His papa had to use his connections to get him to this position. These thoughts went through my head as I studied his beautiful medals that dangled across his chest. They were all different colors- gold, bronze, silver- and they were all attached by ribbons of various colors. He watched me stare at his medals, and he immediately looked down and brushed his hand admiringly over them. "You like MY medals?" he asked, asserting ownership over them. I didn't know if he was trying to be nice and engage me in a conversation or if he was being condescending, so I wasn't sure exactly how to answer.

"Yes, sir" was all I could muster.

He moved his horse until both of them towered over me. His presence was overbearing. I swallowed my saliva down hard. Short, thin arms wrapped around my lower waist. Vibrations shook my body. My sister was trembling in fear and embracing me for safety. I rubbed her head, acknowledging that it would be ok, even though that wasn't my feeling. I knew what this Commander was capable of, and not knowing what he wanted with us really scared me. I was trying to be brave for my sister, so I gently coaxed her to stand behind me. She moved back behind me while keeping her arms wrapped around my waist.

"Where are you going, peasant boy?" he asked in a deep, condescending tone.

"My sister and I are going to visit a neighbor."

He leaned down closer so he could look me more directly in the face, but I was too distracted by his medals. Even on this big, overbearing man, they dangled so daintily from his protruding, muscular chest. I could feel his eyes examining me very closely. They swept over my entire face and down over my body. He laughed while he examined my clothes, but my eyes never left those medals.

Finally, he sat straight up on his horse again and the beast followed suit. Standing there, it looked like a perfect statue was right in front of me. He slowly picked up one of his medals and looked at it admiringly. "Do you know how I won this particular one?"

"No, sir," I said.

"I got this for gutting the life out of a stupid peasant boy like you," he said in a scathing tone.

"Beating defenseless peasants doesn't make you a hero worthy of a medal," I snapped back at him. To this day, I still don't know what came over me. I just felt he needed to be put in his place and even as a young teenager; I was the one to do it.

He jumped off his horse immediately and peeled my sister off of my waist. I remember his fist charging angrily towards my stomach as I stood there waiting for the impact. Gasping helplessly for air, I fell hard to the ground and into the fetal position to try and ease the pain. My soul felt detached from my body like I was physically there but spiritually I was somewhere else. The laughter from Borzniov and his men faintly rang through my ears. I somehow managed to turn my head up a little to see him jump on his horse. He looked down upon me. His eyes burned from the devil's fire and pierced through my soul.

"Until the day you die, you'll always be a worthless peasant boy." HUHHHHHHPPPHHHHHH, he collected as much saliva as he could muster in his mouth and released it right onto me. He charged off with his men following close behind him.

When the sounds of the horses' hooves were no longer audible, my sister rushed over to my side. "Georgi, Georgi," she said as she gently shook me.

Slowly, my energy came back to me. I sat up very slowly and breathed in and out continuously until inhaling and exhaling required no exerted energy from me. I turned to my sister and smiled faintly at her. "I'll be fine, Oksana. Don't worry about me." My attention drew out to the horizon and thoughts raced into my head as to why he hadn't killed me. I was lying on the ground, writhing in pain and completely useless. He could have easily killed me, whether by a weapon or strangling me with his bare hands. There was no way I could fight back. He wouldn't or couldn't, which I didn't know.

My mind couldn't help but wander back to the image of those eyes. All I saw was pure evil. Maybe I had seen one of Satan's helpers or even Satan himself.

That was the moment that changed the rest of my life. It was like I had a glimpse of the future, the battle between good and evil. I felt that it was the devil's work trying to relegate me into staying in the life of poverty I was born into, but something deep in me knew that God had shown me this evil as a catalyst, stirring me to action to do something more.

I stood up and brushed my clothes off. I grabbed my sister's hand and smiled at her. "Come on. Let's go to Mrs. Morislav."

JOURNEY OF FATE

One week later from my harrowing encounter with Commander Borzniov, I packed to leave home to try and be conscripted into the army. It was the hardest thing I've ever had to do, well at least at that point in my life it was. Carefully, I placed the few material possessions I had neatly into an old sack. My mother sat quietly on a chair and just watched me. My papa had taken my sister outside. He claimed he didn't want her to get upset, but I know my mother wanted to be alone with me. As much as a papa loves his children, nothing was stronger than the bond of a mother and her male or female child. After all, it was the mother who carried the child in her womb, right under her heart. The child and she were one for nine whole months. This created an indescribable bond as a result of that, and it remains for the rest of both of their lives. This was probably why my mother was so distressed at my leaving and caused the conflicted state I was in. I loved my family more than anything, but I knew there was something bigger in store for me. Family was the most important thing in my life.

So, when I was finished packing, I looked up at my mother and saw tears rolling down her face. It cut my insides like a knife.

I walked over and sat on the cot next to her. We sat in silence just staring at the wall ahead of us. Suddenly, I felt her hand on top of mine. Both of us turned to look at each other. "Please, don't go Georgi. I know I haven't provided much for you, but I try. I try so hard...so hard and somehow I can never make enough. I'm sorry, but please don't leave. Especially, please don't join the military, please."

"Mama, don't blame yourself for my leaving. I know you do your best, but I have to go."

"You know what they do to boys from poverty. They'll assign you to the most dangerous tasks." She lost control over her tears and they began to flow violently down her cheeks. "I can't bear to lose my only son." She looked down toward my necklace. "And what if they find out that you are..."

I quickly took my necklace off and walked over to put it in my bag. "No one must ever know, mama. Please, never!"

She shook her head begrudgingly in agreement and stroked my face. I think she knew that this would be the last time I would see her. "I love you so much and I'm going to miss you," she said as she hugged me. I had to forcibly tear myself away from her. Grabbing my sack, I turned around to look at her for the last time. She never looked back at me. Her tears kept streaming down her face as she stared directly ahead at the wall. Had she watched me take up all my belongings and head out the door, she would not have let me leave. She would have stood in the doorway begging me not to go. Since she knew how much I wanted this, she just sat down and tried to contain her emotions.

Outside, my papa and my sister waited for me. I walked up to my papa, who extended his hand for a shake. I knew I would never get a hug from my papa or any type of loving emotion. It was as if there was an unwritten rule somewhere saying papas can't show loving emotion toward their sons. That is why I was so glad when I had a daughter of my own. I couldn't imagine not being loving towards any child. Of course, a papa wants his son to grow up to be tough and manly. A little affection shouldn't hurt the manliness of a son. With a daughter, it's wonderful not to worry about showing too much affection. I looked my papa straight in the eye and sternly shook his hand.

My sister was staring at my sack, deeply confused. "Georgi, what is that?"

I tried to find the easiest way to tell her I was leaving and never coming home again, but how can you really tell your baby sister you will never see her again? "I'm going away for a while, Oksana."

"Where are you going?"

"Some place far."

"Why?"

"There's something I have to do."

"What?"

I laughed and shook my head. Children are naturally curious and pester you until they get an answer that is satisfactory for them. I wouldn't tell her I was going to join the military, where I could be seriously injured or even killed. She didn't need to be corrupted by tales of violence. I wanted her to maintain her adorable innocence for as long as she could, before the harsh realities of the world hardened her. "Just promise me you'll be a good girl; that you'll listen to mama and papa and won't cause them any problems. I expect to hear a good report about you, understood?"

She sadly gazed into my eyes. The tears swelled in her eyes, causing me to embrace her in a tight hug. I stroked her soft silky hair and breathed in to remember her sweet scent. I stayed like this for a few moments to etch this memory in my mind so I would have it during difficult times. Believe me, it was needed in the years to come. Separating from her was a struggle for me. I headed out toward the horizon, but stopped to turn around. I had to look one last time at the home I had lived in my entire life. The frail little shack that looked like it could fall apart at any moment was a big part of who I was. That house and that life was an old comfortable shoe for me and now I was headed into the great unknown. What would happen to me and what would my future be? Little did I know as I walked toward the horizon, just how big an impact my decision to leave home and join the military would have on the future of the world...?

MONGOLIAN BATTLE

All my difficult years of training, reading, and studying military tactics led me to this point in 1939. Having transformed from a timid young teenager into a seasoned military mind, I was now fully equipped with knowledge and a prophetic nature I felt could help me lead my men into any battle. The Japanese were approaching our borders through Mongolia and had to be stopped. Premiere Stalin had ordered war games to be carried out to determine who would lead our troops into Mongolia to fight the enemy. I was pitted against a man who I had greatly admired, General Dmitry Pavlov. He had just returned from commanding our tank brigades in the Spanish Civil War over in Spain. He also bravely served in our Civil War in the earlier part of the century.

I was led into a room by a Commander and seated at a table containing a map of Mongolia. Directly across from me was General Pavlov himself. His cold dark eyes stared right through me, but the only thing I could concentrate on was his completely bald head. The room was very dark except for a lamp that shone on the map. The little bit of light caught his bald head and it gleamed. He briskly stood up and shook my hand. It wasn't a warm handshake, as he gripped my hand hard. It was more of an intimidation tactic on his part. I sat down in my chair and studied the map.

"Zhukov, you are going to portray the Soviet army and Pavlov will be the Japanese. You will write down your tactics on how you plan to defeat the enemy. Please begin now," said the Commander.

My eyes cascaded over the map, studying where the enemy was and the borders where my army would approach from. I picked up my pencil and quickly jotted down on the paper. My mind raced through all the strategies I had learned from all the way back in military school as well as what this enemy was like. I quickly jotted down onto the paper my plans. I could hear Pavlov furiously writing, glancing up at me curiously every once in a while to study my expression. I kept on my task, completely stoic in my expression.

"Time!" the Commander yelled. I put down my pencil and handed my paper to the Commander. Pavlov did the same. The Commander read Pavlov's paper and drew out exactly his tactics as he described he would carry out as if he were the Japanese General. Then, he read my paper and drew out my tactics as I would lead the Soviet army. He quickly dropped his pencil and looked up at me. "This is incredible. Zhukov has won the game!" the Commander had announced. Pavlov was taken aback. He was so shocked that when I went to shake his hand, he reciprocated with a limp grip apparently in a daze.

I had done so well in this game that Stalin himself assigned me to lead the fight against the invasion of the Japanese into Mongolia. The exact tactics I wrote on that paper I put to use in the actual battle.

At the time, I knew this fight against the Japanese would have major implications, but I wasn't sure exactly how. My good friend

Commander Yegorov was there to assist me and apprise me of the current situation so I could make plans of how to proceed.

One early evening, I stood at the opened flap of my tent studying the actions of the enemy. We had set our tent up on the outskirts of where the current battle was being fought. I had read about the Japanese and their fighting methods before, but I felt it was also important to study the incumbent General's actions and habits in person.

That particular evening, I was studying the two Japanese Generals who were heading this attack- Himoshira and Yokomoto. I had studied these two very carefully and knew what drove their actions. Himoshira was born into a military family. One of his family members served in every war the Japanese were involved in. It was important for him to bring honor to his family name, and that meant he would stop at nothing to lead this ferocious offensive and kill all the Soviet soldiers in sight by himself if his men couldn't do it. Yokomoto came from the opposite type of situation. He came from a poor family and joined the military to escape it, similar to my background. He had worked his way up and felt he had to prove himself worthy of this high military honor bestowed upon him by the Japanese military. Even though the two came from completely divergent backgrounds, they shared the Japanese sentiment toward the Soviets. They felt the Soviets were ignorant people, not capable of matching the intense ferocity with which the Japanese fought with. I smiled to myself thinking of this and how it was the perfect sentiment with which to trap them.

Through my binoculars, I watched the two of them laughing. Yokomoto had a manual in his hand and the two were pouring over it- pointing at parts and laughing. While I watched, I had to adjust my jacket. Even though the battle had wound down for the day and I could have changed into something more comfortable for dinner, I believed that a Commander should always be dressed in his full military uniform and boots. As we approached the nighttime, it was getting cooler. The sweat that seeped through my uniform reminded me just how hot the day had been. I was thinking of the heat when Yegorov interrupted me.

"Marshal Zhukov, are you ready to examine this?" I ignored him for a moment, while I continued to look through the binoculars and watch the two men examine the manual. "Do you think they found the manuals you spread out?"

"The one entitled "What the Soviet Soldier Must Know in the Defense? What do you think I'm watching now? Two flies getting ready to land in a big spider web, that's what I see." I started to laugh at how incredibly gullible they were. Did they really think we were inept enough to leave our real battle tactics strewn around on the field? Actually, yes they did think that. That's why I did it.

Yegorov roared in laughter. "Sir, they are going to get a big surprise!"

I dropped my binoculars and turned to him. I grinned at his statement. Anxiously, I made my way over to the map to plan out this spider web of a trap for our enemy. "We are here right now," I said pointing to the map. "I want to make it seem like we are retreating further north. We have to act defensively, like we're the victims. You understand, play off their mentality towards us. But while this is going on, we're going to switch to the offensive. We're going to draw our troops from the north, west, and south and completely surround them." I was wildly pointing at places on the map with my hands, demonstrating what we were going to do. I had always been very animated when discussing strategy, so much so that my hands always flew all over the place when I spoke. "How many troops are in each of these regiments?" I asked as I pointed to them on the map.

Yegorov looked at the spots where I was pointing and became flustered. "I'm not exactly certain as to how many men are in each unit," he said. He worriedly looked up to see my reaction to this piece of information.

I could feel my face grow red and my heart beating quickly. My anger boiled below the surface like a volcano ready to explode. I was planning a major attack and needed to be entirely accurate on every aspect of the troops. "Isn't that your job to know all this information? If I ask you a question relating to the troops, then I expect an accurate answer!" I took a deep breath for a moment, trying to control my usually quickly, escalating anger. "I want you to ride out to the troops and take an inventory of everything- how many men in each regiment and the weapons they have and what more they need. Do you understand me?"

"Yes, sir," he saluted me with a relieved look on his face, content that I didn't lash out at him too much for his deficiencies in apprising me of the situation.

Before he headed outside the tent, I stopped him. "Yegorov!" He stopped and turned to me. "Do this as quickly as possible. I want to attack early morning on Sunday."

"Sunday, sir?" He asked, seemingly confused.

"Do you honestly think they'll be ready for a major attack when they're dreaming of what fun activities they're going to do on their day off?" I mischievously smiled at him.

He laughed and headed out of the tent. I heard Yegorov gallop off on his horse, headed out to the troops to get a better grasp of the situation, while trying to get back into my good graces.

The next few days, our planes would bomb the enemy at night to drown out the movement of our troops closer to the area.

The Japanese were bright and observant people and I wanted to throw them off course by distracting them. Of course, I didn't sleep for days. I constantly stood at the opening of the tent with the binoculars, watching the bombs explode. Large columns of fire and smoke lit up the night sky and the heat from the blasts warmed the cool night. The Japanese ferociously attacked us, and we fought hard to defend ourselves. The planes had performed an exhaustive effort of their bombings, and it was clear to me that the Japanese had matched that with their full strength of an onslaught. Numerous Soviet planes had been shot down and it appeared that we were at the end of our rope. To the Japanese, victory was imminent for them. That was right where I wanted them.

On the Sunday of our impending attack, everything was silent. This was the calm before the storm. I peered out over the Japanese camp. Almost everyone was asleep except for two men who were probably on shift to guard the camp and keep an eye out. They were fairly silent between the two and just looking out over the land. Every once in a while they appeared to exchange words, but other than that, they just looked out onto the silent land. Dawn was quickly approaching and I knew that this was the moment I had been waiting for. I dropped my binoculars and turned to Yegorov who was sitting in a chair drinking some tea. "It's time. I'm going to ride out and alert the troops on the outskirts. You tell them to begin firing the artillery and push the line north."

Before he could respond, I quickly put on my cap and set out to mount my horse. I had to sneak around the tent carefully, so as not to be discovered. My dark bay horse was standing at full attention like he knew he was going to be ridden for a very important mission. He stood patiently as I placed the saddle gently on his back. I stroked his beautiful thick coat that was the color of dark chocolate. He was a monstrous beast standing well taller than all the other horses. It was important for a Commander to have an overbearing beast of an animal to ride to show status and instill more respect from the men you were leading into battle. With an exhausting thrust, I pushed myself on top of the horse. "YA, YA," my horse bolted forward and we were galloping full steam ahead. The air hitting my face felt like needles penetrating my skin. We were moving so fast that our surroundings were blurred. And even though the wind was whipping past my ears, the sound of artillery fire pierced through this shield.

I could see the men lined up in the distance and when I drew closer to them, I yelled, "Attack, attack. Let's get moving."

Quickly, I galloped my horse back towards the artillery front. The wind whipped again, and the smell of smoke filled my nostrils and went into my lungs. I was a crazed man, the anxiety and anticipation of seeing my plan unfold before my eyes was the cause of it. Either my horse was nervous from everything going on or he felt my same thrill of exhilaration, because he surged forward at much greater speed without my forcing him to. His nostrils flared and his grunting grew louder and louder as we covered more ground.

"Whoa, boy," I quickly stopped him as we reached our headquarters. He came to a sliding stop and shook his head wildly, expending excess energy he had from our thrill ride. I pulled out my binoculars to watch what was happening on the field. My men charged mercilessly at the enemy. I could see their fiery intensity even through my binoculars. Back and forth firing from both sides ensued, until I noticed my men were going down at an alarming rate.

Looking over to the Japanese side, I saw a large group of Japanese soldiers coming from the west straight at our side. They fought as if they didn't care if they lived or died. These new Japanese soldiers joined the men we had surprised and in overwhelming us, our men began to retreat. Anger consumed my whole body, and my face was growing red. Taking my frustration out on my horse, I kicked his sides with all the strength in my legs. He immediately jolted forward, almost causing me to lose my balance. I gripped his sides tightly with my legs as the wind whipped past my face. I didn't take my eyes off of my men. "What the hell are you doing? Anyone who retreats will be trampled by my horse!" I growled at them. "Get in there and fight! We have to distract them a while longer," I urged them on. I galloped up and down the lines to make sure these men charged at the enemy with full intensity.

One man had been holding back and started to move backwards away from the fighting. Keeping my eye firmly on my target, I violently galloped my horse up to him. He saw me coming and cowered away from my path. I stopped my horse abruptly, just inches away from him. He shakily looked down at my horses large hooves and slowly examined the animal all the way up to the top. He looked up at me with tremendous fear in his eyes. He was sweating profusely. I looked down at him. "If you don't take that gun and fight like a real Soviet soldier, you are going to feel fifteen hundred pounds of animal flesh crush every bone in your body!" He grabbed his gun and ran back to the front line.

Out in the distance, the air was rumbling. I looked back and could see the planes swooping in. Within a few minutes, the bombs were being dropped. Now, my offensive plan was being implemented. The Japanese were dropping like flies, but they weren't letting up in their intensity and fighting to the death ideology. As the bombs dropped, I made my way back towards the tent, trying to avoid being hit by a bomb. The plan was being executed perfectly. The planes stopped the bombing and flew away to make it appear as if the assault had stopped. I knew it was time to unleash our final assault.

The ground was shaking and I smiled, consumed with excitement at what was to come next. The enemy was right where we wanted them, as all the Japanese troops had congregated together at this point to concentrate their attack on us. As the ground violently shook, I looked back towards the east where our front line was. Behind my men, the tanks began to roll in and fire on the Japanese. They gave one last thrust forward upon my men. The back and forth continued as the Japanese were dropping like flies at an alarming rate. The men who were left were firing at us, knowing their death was imminent. As the tanks from the east drew in closer, the tanks came in from the west, behind the Japanese. They were being fired on from either side. They tried to spread themselves to the north and the south to avoid the onslaught. To the north, our tanks were making their way in. They were hunting down these Japanese who were trying to spread themselves in different directions. If someone were looking at this battle from a distance, the look of panic on the Japanese faces spoke more than a thousand words ever could.

We had them now completely encircled. They knew it was the end of their effort here in Mongolia. Dropping their weapons, they held up their arms. The white flag of surrender was being waved, and this was my signal to make my way over to accept. When I reached the two Generals, I got off my horse and acknowledged them. They handed me their white flag, symbolizing an agreement of surrender. I turned around to look at all my men and nodded my head. Even through their exhaustion, they could not hide their enormous excitement over their tremendous effort. The men waved their guns in the air as they cheered loudly. Those who were in the tanks made their way outside to join the ground forces in the celebration. I made my way around, shaking their hands and patting them all on the backs in celebration of this wonderful victory. The troops began to chant something faintly, until more men joined in and I could understand what they were saying, "Zhukov, Zhukov, Zhukov, Zhukov."

I looked over at the Japanese Generals to see their reaction to this. Yes, I admit it was out of arrogance. They stood stone faced watching our celebration. Their faces tried to hide their frustration of defeat, but their eyes couldn't. I knew that this was an important victory for our country, but I wouldn't realize just how important until events would unfold later. My eyes followed the two Generals as they made their way back into their tent. I couldn't see exactly what they were doing, so my curiosity made me sneak up to the outside of the tent. I was now able to peer inside through the open flap without being detected.

In the tent, Hiroshima and Yokomoto dropped down in their chairs. They were silent for a few moments, until Yokomoto interrupts. "I have to tell him our plan failed." Hiroshima looked up horrified and fearful. "He'll be so angry..." He seemed to ponder for a moment about his own thought in his head and then looked back at Yokomoto. He finally nodded in agreement. Yokomoto walked slowly towards the phone on the table, like a prisoner on a death walk slinks toward his executioner. He picked up the phone and worked his fingers around the numbers. He took a deep breath and exhaled slowly. "We have officially surrendered to Marshal Zhukov and the Soviets."

THE BEGINNING OF OUR
WORST NIGHTMARE

When I returned to Moscow, I was lauded as a hero. I enjoyed the constant admiration I received. I couldn't walk through the streets without someone coming up to me and expressing their gratitude. Parades and events were going on to celebrate the victory. The Soviet people mistakenly thought all our troubles were over and were lured into a false sense of security. All this happiness and celebration was merely a facade which was covering up the horrors and the suffering that was happening behind closed doors. A foreign threat was the least of our problems compared to what was going on in our own country.

My good friend Yegorov, who despite his short comings, was an excellent Commander. One would think he would be rewarded and lauded for his exemplary work, but a completely opposite fate awaited him. This is the story I heard from someone who was there the night his fate was handed down.

Premiere Stalin was seated at his desk. He was an overbearing figure, an almost perfect image of what a dictator should look like. He had a hardened exterior that was complimented by cold, big round dark eyes that could pierce through you. All the leaders of the past used their facial hair to symbolize their status and strength, and Stalin chose to continue this honored tradition. His big, bushy, thick, dark moustache was a menacing sight on his face. It also distracted you from the deep smallpox scars that marred his face. Every time he looked in the mirror, these deep, accented marks served as a reminder of his difficult and unloving childhood. He never learned warmth and compassion from family, only the stinging of leather as his papa's belt would hit his flesh.

While reading a paper, he was interrupted by a knock at the door. "What is it?" Stalin snapped, angered to be interrupted.

The door opened slowly, and it was Lavrentiy Beria. This bald, stout, sniveling, pathetic excuse for a man was Stalin's lap dog. "Premiere Stalin, we have the prisoner," he says in an obedient manner.

Stalin's eyes lit up in pleasure, while maintaining a cold, icy stare. "Get him in here now."

Beria walked out of the office, and moments later led in two of his secret policemen who hung on to each of Yegorov's arms as he was handcuffed behind his back. They pushed him violently onto the floor, and he fell severely on his left arm. Stalin rose from his seat to walk in front of him, as Yegorov was struggling to prop himself up onto his knees. Stalin chuckled to himself as he watched this pathetic sight of this once proud General at his mercy. Yegorov was fighting with himself so as not to shake in front of Premiere Stalin, but he was filled with great trepidation. Stalin looked down at him and spoke.

"These documents have come to my attention about you. And do you know what they're relating to?"

"I don't know, sir," Yegorov quietly said.

Stalin's anger boiled within him, like lava building up inside a ready to explode volcano. He grabbed the papers off his desk and shoved them within an inch away from Yegorov's face. He rippled the papers with his thumb, as Yegorov nervously watched. "These papers tell me you were acting as a spy for the Japanese while in Mongolia and now, according to my reliable German sources, you are organizing a coup to overthrow me," Stalin said disturbingly calm.

Yegorov looked up at Stalin, horrified from his accusations. "Premiere Stalin, I've never associated myself with the Japanese. Marshal Zhukov can attest to that fact," he said trying to hold back tears. "And I swear to you I'm not involved in any coup against you. I don't know who's telling you this, but it's not true. I swear to you!"

Now, the volcano exploded within Stalin. "You're lying! Beria, make him admit to what he's done!"

Beria grabbed a wooden plank and strode over behind Yegorov. He raised the plank up high over his head. Yegorov was anxiously waiting, not knowing what would happen to him. Beria, like a black widow spider who had its innocent fly ensnared in its web, watched his prey for a moment. Then, with all the force in his body, he struck Yegorov in the back. The impact from this blunt object knocked the wind out of him. Yegorov fell to the ground, and struggled to breathe. Beria continued to beat him a few more times with the plank. Yegorov was squirming on the floor like a helpless worm, his arms still tied behind his back. Beria kicked him, alternating between his stomach and his head. Blood was streaming out of his nose and out of his mouth.

"Enough!" Stalin halted him before he killed Yegorov. He kneeled down above Yegorov. "Now is there anything you want to admit?"

Yegorov was heavily wheezing. The pain was shooting through his limp body. He struggled to slowly look up at Stalin. "I won't admit to something I didn't do. I couldn't live with myself if I did that," he said slowly and quietly, still trying to catch his breath.

"Then you won't live! Take him out and kill this traitor swine!"

The two secret policemen grabbed Yegorov, who was too weak to stand on his own. They dragged him out, Beria led the way and Stalin followed close behind. They arrived outside at a single wall. Policemen with rifles were standing in a line several yards away from the wall. Yegorov was too weak to stand, so he leaned up against the wall. He faced straight ahead and stared at the guns that were all pointed at him.

Stalin walked behind the officer's shooting line so he could watch. "Do you have any last words?"

Yegorov tried to fight back the tears, thinking of this unjust end to his life. He managed a sudden rejuvenation of his energy, as if God knew the truth and was allowing him to give his own last rites. "I am an honest soldier, dedicated to the Party, the State, and the people. My whole life has been spent in selfless and honest work before the Party and its leaders. I shall die with words of love for you, the Party and the country, and with a boundless faith in Communism. Long live Stalin and…" Gunshots rang out before he could finish. Blood flew from his body as the bullets enter his already weak and fragile torso. He fell to the ground with a loud thud. The pool of blood grew as the life slowly drained out of him.

Stalin marched back to his office with Beria in tow. He sat back down at his desk and continued working through the papers. He picked up the paper that was in front of him and examined it. "Marshal Georgi Zhukov, what are we going to do with you?" He is interrupted by Beria trying to clean the blood stains off the floor. "Leave that," Stalin ordered. "I want others who come in here to be reminded of what happens to traitors."

Beria and Stalin smiled at each other, a mutual and unspoken understanding between the two about the murder that had been carried out.

Stalin had executed most of our top Commanders and almost all our Marshals. I, Marshal Georgi Zhukov, was the only Marshal he had kept alive. I never really knew why, but I assumed it was because of my success in Mongolia. These actions of Stalin, which caused a significant attenuation of our military strength, scared me, and now even more so with what were staring at me on my desk. On my desk, were warnings about the devil I spoke of earlier and the one who haunted me from the time of the war with Japan, Adolf Hitler and his army.

In keeping with my method of knowing your enemy really well, I managed to acquire a copy of Hitler's book *Mein Kampf.* So far, all of Hitler's prophecies were coming true. France had fallen into his hands. One aspect of the book that disturbed me was his hatred towards Communism. I knew he wanted to conquer the Soviet Union, as one of his major conquests in his goal of ruling the entire world. What I had accomplished in defeating the Japanese was their refusal to join the Germans in invading the Motherland, which would have created an undefeatable force. The Japanese chose not to challenge me once again, and instead took the war on the west by attacking the Americans at Pearl Harbor in 1941. While I felt incredibly sorry for the Americans having an unprovoked attack raged upon them, I knew if the Japanese had joined the Germans in invading our Soviet Union, the consequences would have been much more severe.

Right then, before me, were the warnings that Hitler and his army were breaking through the border into the Soviet part of

Poland. Stalin ignorantly had signed the Non-Aggression Pact with Hitler the year before, in which Poland was divided and the Germans would not be allowed to invade our part of that country. Hitler completely disregarded this as I knew he would. The British tried to appease this mad man with a similar pact and look what it got them, almost saying "Heil, Hitler."

I had to warn Stalin that the army needed to be prepared for an imminent attack from Nazi Germany. Since Stalin murdered most of our good personnel, the army had been in shambles. There were no experienced leaders to organize our men and lead them into battle. That's why we needed extra time to prepare. What if I did tell Stalin that the Non-Aggression Pact was meaningless and his efforts were futile? I could end up like Yegorov and all the other Commanders whose blood lay on Stalin's hands. Out of frustration, I buried my head in my hands. I listened to the clock slowly ticking away a few feet from me. A very uneasy feeling suddenly came over me.

"You have to tell him," a voice pleaded. I picked my head up and looked around the room, but nothing was there. My heart beat furiously, as I looked frantically to find out who or what had spoken. "You are the great Marshal Zhukov and he will listen to you," the voice said again. I sprung out of my chair, at this point very angry.

"Who the hell is there?" The room temperature suddenly dropped and I could sense something behind me, watching me. I slowly turned around to see a faint white specter. I immediately recognized it was my dead comrade Yegorov. My eyes grew wide in fear. Was he really standing before me or was I hallucinating from exhaustion? I was frozen in place while I stared at him; the fear consumed me.

"I see you got the intelligence report," he said.

"Yes."

"Do you really know why I was killed? Why all of us were killed?" I merely shook my head no. "Stalin got his hands on some report that all of us, me included, were conspiring with the Japanese government to overthrow him." Yegorov stopped and looked at the clock before continuing. "That information came from Hitler himself."

Like a bolt of lightning had struck me, the realization hit me as to what was going on. I ignored for a moment that I was speaking to a dead man.

"Oh my God, I thought! He purposely did it to weaken our army even further. What better way than to play into Stalin's power hungry paranoia?"

"To make matters worse, Stalin gave the Germans permission to enter our land, something about looking for a lost regiment that had wandered from their part of the Polish border."

"He gave them permission to go onto our land? Has he completely lost his mind? They're scouting our land and positions so they can prepare an attack on us."

"That's why you have to be the one to alert him. He'll listen to you," said Yegorov's specter.

"He'll kill me!" I cried out. I then thought to myself what if my angering Stalin makes him investigate me more and he finds out my secret.

"It's something you have to do."

The clock chimed and I raised my head from my hands, still sitting at my desk. I looked around the room, but Yegorov was gone. I rubbed my eyes and shook my head. Once again, I looked around. Still, he was nowhere in sight. The room was eerily silent, confirming the emptiness before my eyes. The feeling someone was watching me was gone and the room had returned to a normal temperature. Had I fallen asleep and he came to warn me from beyond the grave in my dream? This experience deeply concerned me, so I decided to head out for a walk to organize my thoughts. Maybe the fresh air would help me sort through my confused state.

On that dreary and overcast afternoon, the somber mood of the atmosphere didn't help clear my confusion. In fact, my mind wildly raced. I first thought about Yegorov and the false accusations against him. Almost all of our good Commanders had perished at the hands of that paranoid Stalin. Our army lacked the necessary leadership to prevail in an imminent fight with Germany. Yes, Germany. All these actions lately were organized by Hitler himself. I was certain of it. Was Stalin really that oblivious to Hitler's intentions and so give Hitler permission? How could he just grant permission to go onto Soviet soil? Stalin had to have known about the underlying reason for the German invasion. If he really was unaware of all this or he didn't want to believe it then someone really did need to tell him. Why me? I thought once again about Yegorov and how he died. I heard stories about the others' deaths, their grizzly ends, and how they had to face their murderers staring straight at the rifles that would fill them with bullets and leave them to writhe in pain...

Laughter filled the air. It was the laughter of children. I turned around to find I had walked to a garden where children were playing. One little girl in particular caught my eye. She was running around with two little boys, without a care in the world. Her long dark hair flowed gently in the breeze. This little girl evoked memories of my little sister. I remembered her sweet and gentle ways. It's amazing how there can be such evil and yet the innocence of a child reminds you that there is some good left in the world. Even on this overcast day, the sun decided to appear for a few moments. The light shined on the little girl's beautiful hair, almost like a sign from God. That sight almost made me forget my troubles, but when the sun retreated back behind the clouds, it brought the anxiety of my decision back to me. I was facing a three headed monster straight on- the threat of a massive attack and us not being ready, potential imminent death from defying Premiere Stalin, and my own internal conflict of doing what was right for the Motherland or trying to save my own life. Here I was, the lone slayer, needing to win the battle against the monster as a whole. Which head of the monster would I slay first? I started to walk away, but turned around to catch one more glimpse of the children at play. That was the moment I knew what I had to do and I knew time was running out...

STIRRING STALIN TO ACTION

I marched up the numerous steps of the building that housed Stalin's office, with my hat under my right arm. One by one, I placed my foot on the steps. With each step, my legs grew heavier and heavier and my breathing strained more and more. I finally reached the large, overbearing dark oak doors where two guards were standing. "Zhukov to see Stalin," I said.

The two examined my attire, their eyes cascading up and down my light brown uniform. Acknowledging my status as Marshal, they immediately opened the doors for me out of reverence. The big dark oak doors slowly opened and I marched through. The palatial building was an elaborate display of the finest marble and gold. Enormous paintings of the great leaders of the past hang high on the wall and dwarfed even the tallest man. The overwhelming sea of white marble floors flowed past me as I, the warrior, marched to face one head of the three headed monster. Down the hall I walked, my sword of bravery within me, ready to slay this beast.

Just outside Stalin's office was a guard, staring straight ahead until he saw me.

"What is your business here?" he demanded.

I ignored him, strictly focusing my energies on facing the beast. The guard charged right at me, trying to physically restrain me in his grasp until I answered him. I refused to give in to his demand. As he was coming towards me, I glared at him with all the anger that consumed me. He grabbed my arm and with all the force I could muster up, I shoved him forcefully. He landed in the sea of white marble. "Get out of my way," I growled at him. He looked up at me, stunned by the fact that I was able to overpower him. He most likely acted in this way because Stalin would have killed him for not properly guarding his office. At this point, I didn't care. Nothing mattered to me except facing Stalin head on. Now, I wasn't concerned with facing execution for defying him. I knew what needed to be done and felt a higher force was with me.

With all of my strength, I pushed open the heavy doors and marched down the floor towards his enormous desk. He had been writing furiously on papers until he saw me burst through the door. He threw down his pen and lunged out of his chair. "How dare you come in here like that," he growled at me.

I didn't answer him immediately. As I drew closer, the scars on his face appeared deeper and more pronounced to me. His big, dark eyes glared into mine. This was our stand off, and I felt ready for this. With my sword of information and knowledge, I was ready to fend him off. "We have an imminent threat from the Germans. They will attack us. Whether it's tomorrow or a week from now, I don't know. But they will. If they decided to attack us right now, there isn't any way we could defend ourselves. I'm asking you to order that the troops be mobilized to prepare for an attack by the Germans, Premiere Stalin." It ate me up inside to address him in such a formal manner. I had very little respect for him after all he had done.

"Those reports are garbage! You're going to believe the lying, manipulative British?"

"You've seen the reports and haven't done anything about it?"

"Why would I do anything? It's garbage. Hitler and I have an agreement and he intends to honor it."

"The same way he honored his pact with Britain? He's been pushing into our side of Poland, so do you really think he's honoring the pact? He's coming onto our land and preparing to attack us and we must be prepared!"

"You speak of war! Mobilizing troops will provoke them to attack."

"They will attack us regardless! Do you not see what is going on in the world? Hitler hates us and wants nothing more than to see us wiped off the face of the earth. Are you going to stand by and just watch as he murders us? We have to act now! They have a strong, aggressive army who we can't match up against at this moment unless we are prepared. We should have prepared when these warnings came to our attention, but now I'm begging you to take action."

"Get out of my office! I'm not going to be subjected to this nonsense anymore! If I find out you ordered any troop mobilizations, you'll pay."

"Then the blood of the men who die because of those Germans will be on YOUR hands!"

I stormed out of his office, ignoring any response he gave me. While this wasn't exactly what I wanted, I felt I had gotten my point across to him. Now, I had a difficult decision to make. I knew what was at stake both in the context of the impending attack and Stalin's warning to me. If I didn't act, I knew what the consequences would be and they would be far worse than anything Stalin could ever do to me. With time against me, I feverishly stormed down the hall to the military council's meeting room. Bursting through the door, I worked my way around the room to find a pen and paper to write my orders. Like a mad man, I pushed chairs out of the way to get into the desk. The drawer had a tendency to get stuck, so I tugged at it a few times. When it stubbornly refused to open, I gave it one final tug. The drawer gave way and forcefully pushed me back into my chair. I grabbed the paper and pen out of it and tossed the drawer aside, not bothering to put it back in its place. I wrote as quickly and legibly as I could: "To the Military Councils of the Leningrad, Baltic, Western, Kiev, and Odessa Military Districts: A sudden attack is expected by the Germans within the next couple of days. I order our troops along the aforementioned districts to be at full combat readiness. I order the following: the firing points of the regions on the frontier are to be covertly occupied. Before dawn, dispense all aircraft, as well as troops while carefully camouflaging them. Air defense is to have no additional involvement other than being at combat readiness. No other measures are to be taken without specific order."

Before I put the pen to the paper to sign the order, I stopped. I took a deep breath in and held it for a few moments thinking what this entailed. Essentially, I was signing my death warrant if things didn't turn out well. Time was marching on and it was against me. My pen was like a sword and writing my signature on that paper was like a wound to the murderer Stalin. Whether Stalin would come back at me in a vicious attack or acquiesce and crown me victorious was yet to be determined.

I lunged out of the chair and hurried down the hall to the communications office to relay the order. A young officer was consumed by whatever it was he was typing on his typewriter. One by one his fingers hit the large, protruding keys. The tapping sound of the keys hitting the paper grated heavily on my already highly irritated nerves. The officer was so engrossed in what he was doing; he never looked up to acknowledge my presence. I cleared my throat to announce I was there. The officer immediately looked up and bolted straight out of his chair to salute me. He was trying to conceal a look of embarrassment for ignoring me. "Run as fast as you can and deliver this order where I have stated!" I spurred him on.

He took the order from me and read it. "I'm sorry, Marshal Zhukov, but I can't. It's not signed by Premiere Stalin and I need his signature at the bottom to deliver it."

My patience was like a piece of thread that was worn thin and about to snap. "Deliver the order!"

"I'm sorry, sir. I can't."

Just like that, the thread of my patience violently snapped. This pathetic excuse for an officer was defying a higher ranking official's order. He was the last blockade on my road to stirring our armed forces to action. I wasn't going to let him get in my way. From the holster, I swiftly pulled out my gun and held it up to his forehead. In stunned silence, he dropped the order and put his arms up on either side. "Deliver the order or your splattered brain is going to be a decoration for that back wall!"

"Please, Marshal Zhukov, understand that I can't without…"

I unlocked the gun and the clicking sound caused the officer to shake. His eyes grew wide looking into the barrel of the gun. Slowly, I pressed the trigger to release the bullets. "I'm going to tell you one more time to deliver the order!" We were wasting valuable time in this exchange and I wanted nothing more than to get rid of this obstacle.

"Ok, ok. Please don't shoot me," he cowardly pleaded with me. I locked the gun and dropped my arm. He closed his eyes and let out a long sigh of relief. When his eyes opened again and he saw my face, he immediately grabbed the paper and started to dash off. I grabbed his arm. "Tell them to contact me when the operation is carried out." He nodded his head in agreement and darted out the door.

Those hours, sitting there and waiting, were the most excruciating ones I've ever experienced. The clock ticked steadily as the hand made its way around the numbers. This new battle was trying to hold time at bay. As much as you want to be able to stop time, the only way you could win the battle was to be faster than that small second's hand that ticked steadily around the face without fail.

The warrior in me took over. I wasn't going to sit around and wait any longer. I was going to take the initiative and see what actions had transpired. I left the office and rushed down the hall, looking around cautiously to make sure Stalin or anyone else wasn't following me. Once safely outside, the two guards were still in position right at the front doors. They briefly saluted me, and then stood perfectly still once again. I was too busy to acknowledge them. I nervously looked out over the horizon, and I could feel the two guards eyeing me. Below, there were a few people out on the street walking and talking; nothing out of the ordinary. A man and a woman were striding along, holding hands. The man appeared to be in his late twenties, while the woman appeared to be in her late teens. You could tell this was a new relationship by the way they looked at each other. He was much taller than she was, and yet, he looked at her like he worshipped the ground she walked on. She was equally enthralled with her partner. The way she looked up at him with great love in her eyes, like he was the only man for her, warmed my heart. They both looked up and nodded at me, and I reciprocated by smiling.

I had forgotten my dilemma for a brief moment, when I watched the young couple stop and look in horror at something ahead of them. The woman covered her mouth to conceal her horror. I raced down the steps as fast as my portly body would allow me, down to where the two were standing. Straight ahead, the officer I had sent to deliver my orders was covered in dirt and blood. He had been shot in the stomach and blood was soaking through his thick, heavy jacket. As he limped closer to me, I saw his face was scratched up and bloodied. What made my stomach churn was the look of horror on his face. He just stared straight into my eyes as he drew closer, not blinking. He started coughing violently and wheezing uncontrollably. The wheezing grew louder and louder, until he collapsed on the ground. I raced over and kneeled by his side. Coughing up blood from deep within his lungs, he desperately tried to say something to me. Through the wheezing and coughing, he was whispering something that was obviously very important. I leaned down closer and put my ear towards his mouth so I could hear what it was.

"Germans, Germans," he kept repeating over and over.

"What about the Germans?" I tried to gather as much information as I could from him as he grasped for the final moments of his life, but this was a losing battle. He gasped for one final time as the life was sucked out of him. I looked back at the couple who were still standing there in shock, watching this poor officer die in front of their eyes. A noise far out in the distance stunned me. The couple was also looking around to see where the noise was coming from. I stood up to try to see what was causing the noise, but buildings were in my way. I dashed back up the long steps to get a better look. Out in the distance, I watched as fires were burning brightly from numerous spots across the horizon and lit up the night sky. A sound that I will never forget and still haunts me all these years later were the sounds of soldiers screaming in pain and fear from the force of the attack. I hoped my order had been delivered on time and this wasn't really a surprise attack.

Suddenly, rumbling filled the sky. I looked down at the street. People from the buildings were coming out to see what was going on. They were confused and agitated, prancing around to see what the commotion was. BOOM! BOOM! The rumbling from the planes and the exploding of bombs were indicative of the fury being unleashed upon us. People were screaming as the ground rumbled below us. Mothers tried to shield their children from the horror. Papas tried to protect their family while acting as the head of the household by trying to be brave, even though you could sense the fear emanating from them.

I couldn't stand there and watch this anymore. My job was to lead our military and I had to find out what was going on. It was as if I was watching a movie. My trance-like state caused me to believe I wasn't really there. My head swirled as people were running and shoving past me. No one cared or recognized me as an officer of the military. For at that moment, we were all in the same position. It didn't matter if someone was an important politician or a peasant on the street. We all were fighting for survival in the mass hysteria. I made my way pushing through the crowds, still dazed. The streets were packed and it was very difficult to maneuver through, but I continued to push through. I was physically and mentally exhausted, but I knew my men needed me.

While making my way through, a man who was twice as tall as I was shoved past me and knocked me into a wall. My arm was heavily throbbing, and the hard impact against that wall brought me back down to earth and into the current situation. A window was open in front of me and I peeped inside. A woman and her three young children were huddled together on the floor. A man was adjusting the radio in the room. When he was finished, he wrapped his arm around the woman. She gently put her head on his shoulder.

A man's voice came blasting through the radio. The man cleared his throat and then the deep booming voice spoke, "Good evening men, women, and children. This evening, the Germans have attacked the Motherland in an unprovoked manner. This will be taken as an official act of war."

It was like the weight of a two ton truck came crashing down upon me when I heard "official act of war" blasting through the radio. Now it was a reality I had feared for so long- Hitler's hell was now on our soil.

BATTLE BETWEEN HEAVEN AND HELL

Examining the destruction from that night was like taking a trip through hell. Sifting through the damage and destruction was a blow to anyone's psyche. For miles around, there was a field of our planes that had crashed to the ground and still burning. Some were to the point of being unrecognizable. Bodies of the pilots were burnt so badly, there was no way to positively identify them. The smell of charred metal and human remains filled the once fresh air. Body bags were delivered to the sites every day, but the amount of corpses were too abundant for the few bags there were. The bodies were pulled from the planes and stacked up. We were unsure what to do with them and the dilemma we faced weighed heavily on our conscience. Do you just douse and burn them? How could you do that to these poor men and women who already faced a flame induced death? How could their souls ever rest peacefully? Perhaps you just bury them right there on the spot. That would be such an expansive graveyard and a painful reminder of all our failings to prepare for the onset of this war. The buildings nearby were left in shambles. People were buried alive in the rubble. People were wandering around aimlessly, figuring out where to go and what to do next.

I knew what I had to do next. The toll that the tour of destruction took on me was tremendous. I hadn't slept in days, merely being kept awake by the numerous amounts of tea I consumed. It's a peculiar feeling, being physically exhausted and yet being kept awake by a stimulant. You can keep your eyes open but if you dare close them for any reason, including blinking, you will just pass out wherever you are and during whatever you are doing. I must have been an odd site, just keeping my eyes open and staring straight ahead trying to keep my mind focused on the task at hand. I made my way down the hall towards Stalin's office. I was so tired that I was almost unable to push open the gigantic wooden doors. Inside his office, numerous officers were standing around his desk talking at him, sometimes at once. They turned around and stopped in dead silence when they saw me making my way up to his desk.

I was shocked at the sight of Stalin. The feared, evil, and heartless man was now a shell of his former self. It looked like Stalin had killed himself after the vicious attack was unleashed on us and his spirit now took his place to clean up the mess that he helped create. The hair on his head was unkempt and out of place compared to his normal styled and manicured coiffure. His eyes were expressionless, just big black holes that took in an image he looked at and resonated no emotion from his soul. He and I looked into each other's eyes. Those black holes started to suck me in, but in my dazed state I just kept staring. I fought against my exhaustion to clear my dazed state and peel my eyes away from these captors staring at me. I cleared my throat to try and gain his attention.

"They attacked us," Stalin said in a low whimpering voice. I looked up startled that this was such a contrast to his deep and domineering voice. He sounded like a lost, lonely boy who tried to find his way and pleaded for someone to help him. "Hitler and I had an agreement. How could he do this to me and without any warning?"

I sharply looked up and glared at him. This made me so angry! Without any warning, I thought to myself? What the hell was I doing in his office a couple of nights before? Putting on a dancing performance for his amusement? Was I not in this same place shoving warnings in his face and screaming at him to take action? If there had not been men in that office with us, I honestly don't know what I would have done to him. Although, I do admit in my sleepy state I started to day dream about what I would have loved to have done to him.

In the daydream, the warrior in me was stirred to action. I found on his desk the same warning I had shown him and ripped it off his desk. Striding around his desk until I stood directly above him, I grabbed his chair and swung it around until he faced me. Taking the paper, I shoved it in his face. "No warning? No *warning*?!" What the hell do you call this? It was right here on your desk!" When he just sat there looking at me, I screamed at him. "LOOK AT IT!" My blood was boiling in my veins. My anger consumed me. I could feel my eyes bulging out of my head. "This first line, what does it say?" I screamed as I pointed to it.

"Warning about the Germans," he softly mumbled.

"What did you just say? I can't *hear* you!"

He raised his voice and read it again. "Warning about the Germans."

I slammed the paper right on his desk and grabbed the back of his head with a clump of his hair tightly in my fist. I shoved his face directly over that paper. "That was in your hands for weeks and what did you do? You gave the Germans permission to cross over the border from our agreed-on part of Poland, making it easy for them to come in here and get ready to attack us. 'Oh no, they would never do that. We have a pact.' I told you it was all lies and deceit! Now, because you are the most pathetic imbecile excuse for a leader, we've lost many planes and competent pilots all because you didn't take this letter seriously!" I tightened my grip on his hair until I was pulling it out of his head. I slammed his head violently and repeatedly on the letter lying on the desk. "Now, when you face God, you are going to tell him what an incompetent leader you are and why there are hundreds of thousands of dead men lying in piles while the living are trying to decide how to rid themselves of the bodies!" I kept slamming his head down, harder and faster. Repeating this over and over again, I stopped when I heard a loud crack. His skull had sliced down the middle. I released the back of his head and he slumped lifelessly on his desk. Blood was seeping out of his head and right onto that letter. Yes, that letter.

A cough from one of the men standing in the room with us snapped me out of my daydream. I looked at Stalin who was still sitting there in his dazed state. I was very disappointed he wasn't really lifeless over his desk. Then again, there was no one who I felt was able enough to take his place and lead. I certainly wasn't going to do it. Now, I just had to deal with the current state of affairs.

"I'm going to assess the situation and make plans for what we need to do next," I said.

"Yes. Assess," Stalin managed to mutter.

I glared at him; all my anger and emotion were expressed in my eyes. "I'll inform you of my findings."

Back at my house, I tried to concentrate on the task at hand. The map was spread out on a table in the middle of the room. I looked at the enormous size of our country. The extent of it was tremendous. Comparing it to the little country that is Germany was laughable, and yet the monster of this little country had prepared to fight for years and had advanced weapons which caused so much heartache and aggravation. So many Germanys could fit into our vast nation, but the force with which they attacked us further threw our military into shambles. Hitler had most of his forces concentrated in the Motherland. Years later, I learned that by the end of this war, some seventy to eighty percent of German combat forces were destroyed by the Soviet military on the Eastern front. This meant that Hitler had sent even a greater percentage than seventy to eighty percent of his forces to fight the Motherland, leaving the allies to fight only less than fifteen percent.

I thought back to my days in Mongolia, remembering how I knew what the enemy was going to do and how beneficial it was. I knew what Hitler was like, having studied him for a long time, but this attack had depleted us. Like my patience with Stalin, the strength of our military in all aspects was hanging by a thread. All our top commanders with years of battle expertise had been exterminated and now our air force was tattered, and the morale of our troops was low. My mind wandered to the Soviet civilians, until I was interrupted. I imagined standing before me was Hitler himself, even though he really wasn't. It was merely a figment of my imagination that had sprung to life. I had always wanted to meet this monster face to face and delve deeper into his dark, twisted mind. My subconscious seemed aware of this fact and in my delirious state there he stood before my eyes.

Proud as a peacock he stood over the map, staring straight at me. It amazed me how similar Stalin and Hitler appeared, or at least how I perceived them. They both had those deep dark eyes that were like black holes, sucking you in if you looked too deep into them. While Stalin's moustache was bushier and more pronounced, Hitler's still made a statement on his face. It just sat there on his upper lip, short in width and neatly trimmed. His hair was also perfectly styled on top of his head. It seemed evil did share similar physical characteristics. That swastika band rested on Hitler's arm neatly in place, and I couldn't peel my eyes away from it. It was like my soul was resting on a table and that swastika with its sharp edges was coming straight for me, ready to dig its piercing edges through my soul. That symbol wasn't always so bad. I had read somewhere that the Indians in America and the Greeks had used it. Then it was drawn perfectly upright and not a menacing figure in people's eyes. Now, it was bent and twisted like Hitler and the Nazi Party's mentality.

Hitler took his index finger and pointed with great force at a spot on the map. I moved closer until I was standing over it at the opposite end of the table. His finger was pointed directly at Moscow, our capital.

"The heart and soul of your country, that's what I want."

I replied, "Dragging your body through the streets of Moscow is what I want."

Hitler laughed violently. "And how do you plan on doing that? Your army is no match for mine. I have more planes, artillery, tanks and five million men who want to plow through anything on their path to Moscow. When my army meets them, do you know exactly what's going to happen to them?

"No, but I am curious to hear," I said.

"All your food supplies will be destroyed. We're going to blow up any form of transportation to get food into the cities. You're going to watch millions of people starve to death here, here, here," he shouted as he wildly pointed around the map. "Once we reach Moscow, we're going to imprison all the Muscovites while we build massive water ducts around the city," he said pointing all the stress of surprise attacks and trying to desperately be one step ahead of our invaders. Then, I remembered the stories I had read about the great American President Abraham Lincoln. During the American Civil War when the situation seemed bleak and the country was ready to be torn in half, President Lincoln would wander through the hallways of the White House having whole conversations with God about why he was being tested and what he should do. The current circumstances weren't exactly the same, considering a foreign enemy was trying to tear us apart, but we were on the verge of also being torn apart and worse, being annihilated.

Forcing myself to focus, I stayed up the whole night pouring over the map and studying in which direction Hitler's army was headed. I drew a red X over Moscow, like marking the spot on a treasure map. That's what Moscow was like to the Soviet people, a treasure. The rich history of the city, the fact that it was our heart; our political center; and our religious center made it a do or die situation to save the city. Moscow was the Soviet identity. If Hitler took it, then he might as well kill all of us. Death wouldn't hurt nearly as much as the sight of a Nazi flag flying high from the top of one of our beautiful buildings. It would be like a hand digging deep into a Soviet's chest and tearing their heart out from the cage in which it beats steadily and proudly in, and then throwing it on the ground while stomping on it as the blood splatters out with each forceful blow. There the heart lay as black as death on the ground while the Nazi flag flies proudly in the wind. This was motivation for continuing to study our strategy and hold my exhaustion at bay.

The enemy was coming at us from the south, west, and north. In the South, they were going through Kiev to push to Stalingrad. In the west, they were penetrating from Poland where they originally breached the border and were going through Minsk and Vyazma. It was the North part of the attack that would be the deadliest and needing of the most attention for the next few years. Hitler had aligned with the Finnish army against us. Finland bordered us near Leningrad. Now, Leningrad was our focus.

Thinking back to Leningrad, there was a period of time when like President Lincoln you questioned God as to why this was happening and why you were being tested. It didn't matter who you were, you still found yourself questioning the higher power. The pain everyone endured in the coming years was so unbearable; it seemed there was no easy victory to be had. Please God, why are you letting this happen and when would this agony end?

THE TIRELESS MARCH OF
THE NAZIS AND THE SUFFERING
THE SOVIET PEOPLE ENDURED

With relative ease during the years of 1941-1942, the Germans kept pushing through and we were powerless to stop them. Years later, I heard horrific stories coming out of Leningrad. The civilians who were still in the city were terrorized by the enemy. People were randomly shot at as the Germans marched through the city. It didn't matter if they were old or young; they were ravaged by bullets piercing through their bodies. Many years later, I had spoken to a man who had personally witnessed one disturbing account.

The following was how he described it: the echoes of the Germans marching through the streets reverberated off the walls and pavement. While they were marching, they were setting fire to buildings. The Soviet citizens within the city were running out of the buildings trying to escape the fires. Shots rang through the air as the Germans continued to steadily march forward deeper into the heart of the city.

Soviet people were trying to run from the onslaught of the enemy, or at least to prolong their life amidst their inevitable fate of death. There were many women and children moving as quickly as they could but they were no match for the enemy's strength.

A German soldier was running to catch up to a woman who ran with her little girl while holding her hand. "Stop!" the officer shouted. He caught up to them and grabbed the little innocent girl by her pretty blonde hair, dragging her along with such force that he knocked her to the ground.

She was dirty from being on the ground and was shaking from fear of the overpowering man who held her captive. "When I tell you to stop, you better listen or I'll shoot you." Her mother was standing some ten feet away.

She looked on in horror as the officer was manhandling her daughter. "Please don't hurt my little girl," she quietly begged, holding back tears.

"Mommy! Mommy!" she helplessly shouted.

"Shut up, you little brat!" He kicked a puddle of water from the street up into the little girl's face. Her little, puffy, rosy cheeks were tainted by water and dirt.

The mother watched in horror as her little girl pleaded for her safety. She tried to contain her feelings, but not knowing what this German was capable of caused her maternal instincts to explode right out of her, "Please, don't hurt her. You can do what you want with me, but please leave her alone. She's just a child. Please, don't hurt her!" The distress was written all over her face.

The officer grabbed his gun and pointed it at the mother. "Open your mouth one more time, and I swear I will blow your brains out all over the street and your little brat will be cleaning them up."

The mother cried uncontrollably. The tears streamed down her face. She helplessly watched her daughter being manhandled and felt there was nothing she could do except try to appease the German officer.

The German officer stood glaring at the mother and debated whether he should kill her or spare her life. He circled around the little girl as she lay on the ground. He pointed the gun at her and clicked it like he was about to shoot her. "Maybe I should shoot your little brat instead. Yes, one less pathetic Soviet child to deal with."

Silently, the mother prayed to God for the safety of her child, as the officer continued circling around the child. The officer picked up the little girl violently by her hair. He put his arm around her waist and the other arm around her neck, holding her head on the opposite side. "No!" the mother screamed out in horror.

Pushing her hair away from her ear, the officer softly whispered, "Snapping your neck would feel so good."

"I want my mommy," she sobbed. She looked right at her mother with fear mixed with tears.

Her mother was conflicting whether she should act or just hope and pray that the German would finish with her soon and leave them alone. She watched as he continued to play with her daughter's beautiful hair and stroke her head with the gun. Her basic maternal instincts finally drove her to act. She could no longer stand by and watch this man have his way with the only thing she had to live for. She ran toward the officer with all the strength and power her legs could handle. The officer pushed the little girl back down to the ground in order to protect himself. The mother proceeded to attack him, but her strength was no match for his beastly power. He knocked her to the ground and pointed the gun at her.

"I want you to pray for your life!" he shouted at her.

"Please don't kill me. I'm the only one my daughter has in this world. I'm begging you."

The officer laughed at what he felt was a pathetic sight. With the thought in mind of the Soviet inferiority compared to the Germans and how they needed to be destroyed, he clicked the gun and shot the mother right in the head. He marched up to her and continued to spray her with numerous bullets, even though the life had drained out of her long before. He looked up at the people who were wildly fleeing in the distance. He noticed that a smaller crowd had gathered to watch the encounter between him and the mother and daughter. "If any one of you dares to try and cross me, you'll end up like her!" pointing to the mother who was lifeless on the ground in a pool of her own blood. He stormed off to join his other comrades.

The little girl rushed over to her mother. "Wake up, mommy. Wake up," she pleaded as she shook her. The woman's body remained lifeless like a rag doll that was thrown on the ground and forgotten about. Her eyes were wide open and still told the horror of the death she had just experienced. The little girl looked around, helpless and confused. "Help my mommy. Help my mommy," she cried out to the people who were passing by, but not one soul stopped to help her. It was a time of enormous selfishness. Everyone was fighting for their own survival. If someone stopped and helped her, they feared they would be the next victim of the blood thirsty Germans. It was a time when Darwinism rang so true, the theory of survival of the fittest. The little girl was now alone to fend for herself in the cruel and unforgiving world. There were also many other children who were now orphaned.

I understood perfectly well this Darwin theory of the strong surviving, but at the same time I didn't want to feel many years later that there was more that I could have done sooner to help the struggling civilians. That was one of my main reasons for joining the military in the first place, and I wanted to stay true to my word. So, I ordered a major evacuation of the city of Leningrad. Each day, I would mark down at what times they would shell the city. I found that they stopped their activity at eleven at night and started up again at nine the next morning. During the night time hours, we would move as many people as possible out of harm's way. Mostly, women and children were moved out to a safer location. The men stayed behind to fight the onslaught. Families were separated during the darkest hours of our country. The women and children who were evacuated had to trek long distances on their feet. During the evacuations, the background was filled with noise of low humming of the German planes that were coming and swooping in to release the bombs. Whenever the nomads would rest, they would watch the havoc. The planes were like vultures that were waiting up in the air while they dropped the bombs, and then would come in lower to finish off the remains of the dead.

All these people could do was watch. Fear was heavy in the air. Without anything to do but walking and resting, the time was filled by heavy thinking. Where was my husband at that very moment? Was he alive or had he succumbed to these invaders? If he did succumb to them, was it fast or a slow and painful death? What about all those people who were left behind, waiting for their chance to escape the horror? Just how many lives were lost and especially, how many children? How many children were never going to live a complete and fulfilling life? How many would never know what its like to fall in love and get married? How many would never have children of their own to teach the right and wrong way of doing certain things? How many would never see grandchildren and grow old? Even before all that, how ripe enough to be consumed. One woman described to me how she would get bugs to eat. She would comb anxiously through the leaves on the trees. When there was one, she would stop and stand perfectly still. She would watch the little critter move around, completely oblivious to the danger that lurked before it. Her eyes would narrow and focus strictly on this helpless little creature. Very slowly, she would pick her arm up. Her arm was heavy from weakness, but finding a tasty morsel to eat somehow made it easier to deal with the heaviness and lift it effortlessly. As her arm came closer to the bug, she would push her thumb and index finger closer together while keeping them apart so she could pick it up easily. Sometimes the critter would be a wise one and hear her sly movements. She would stop dead in her place while the critter explored its surroundings. When it was satisfied that it was safe from danger, she would continue once again closing in on the bug. When she was hovering above the critter with her two fingers, the thing would usually hear her. Before it could scamper away, she scooped it up with great force. There she held the little thing up to her face and watched it squirm around. She said she felt like a giant spider that had her little bug victim in her beautiful web of death. As she continued to watch the little thing squirm around in fear, she felt sorry for it and considered putting it back down so it could run away. Although you know, that's what she wanted. She wanted to be able to be picked up from the horror that was around her and to be put in another place so she could run away to safety also. Just like the enemy had her and her family in their grasp and were torturing them, she could take no pity on this bug. When her stomach violently growled as she looked at the bug, it reminded her how she needed to have some nutrient. Without hesitation, she lowered the critter into her open, welcoming mouth and when she felt it squirming on her tongue, she tightly closed its only escape to freedom. She moved it so her sharp teeth could dig into its outer covering and let the juices squirt out to meet her appreciative saliva. Swallowing the remains was the most satisfying feeling as it made its way down her throat and into the emptiness of the pit that was her stomach. It was ironic to her how she was being hunted and yet she turned into the hunter and killed innocent little bugs that caused people no harm. It was necessary for the sake of survival.

Back in Leningrad, the planes flew away giving a false reprieve for awhile. People tried to regroup themselves and gather their thoughts to plan what their next step was. There was no place for them to go. Their homes were destroyed and there was no refuge. Buildings were tattered and torn apart, diminished to nothing but rubble. So many people were left to wander the street, helplessly searching and looking up to heaven for an answer, but God was once again absent when the planes came swooping in with more ferocity than before. Young and old alike were scrambling away from the deafening and powerful explosions only to be knocked on the ground. Blood trickled down their ears due to their ear drums bursting from the cacophony of bombs. Whatever building was left standing, the planes blew them to unrecognizable pieces.

To the shock and horror of those who were watching on the ground, the mighty and vital food storage building exploded. Amidst all the confusion, these people stopped dead in their tracks. In slow motion, the fears of everyone came true. Their only source of food vanished right in front of them. All anyone could do at that point was to think about which fate awaited them first- starvation or being killed by bomb or gun.

Inside hospitals, nurses were scurrying to get their patients to safety before a bomb hit the building. They were running frantically from room to room, finding anyone they could. While the explosions continued, nurses tried with all their strength to lift people out of their beds. Sometimes they were unable to do this because they were too ill or not strong enough. There at a crossroad, the nurse would have to choose who would at least have a chance to live and who would have to be left behind to die. Hospitals were filled with young and old, some with minor injuries and others who were on their death beds. It sounds so simple to just take those who barely had injuries and who were sure to live, but is it right to let someone on their death bed be taken by hell's fire? They deserved to be met with a dignified death and not stare into the face of the devil.

Our soldiers, who were fighting other enemy divisions that had advanced beyond the city of Leningrad onto their path toward Moscow, were being met with heavy artillery fire. Back and forth, the fight continued on either side. When the Germans would get a leg up in the fighting, our troops were able to pound right back and for longer. When our troops eased off, the Germans would come back with even greater force. Men on either side were dropping at an alarming rate. Every time artillery fire was heard, many men would scream out in pain and drop to the ground. This fighting went on for several long and arduous minutes until our side ran out of ammunition. Unfortunately, our troops were not well supplied during the early fighting and Stalin was to be blamed for that as well. The shock of the attacks on us left us with little time to fully assess how many weapons and ammunition were needed to effectively fight the enemy. When the attacks significantly eased, the soldiers on the front and everyone in Leningrad who had miraculously survived the attacks just dropped to the ground and looked up to the sky to pray to God. You just wanted an answer or some sort of sign that this suffering would soon stop, but nothing was there but a devastated city with little left standing. It wasn't just the buildings in shambles; it was the will and spirit of the people that was broken. How after all this devastation could they be willed on to fight for their survival? That was the challenge I had to overcome in the coming months.

PRESENT DAY 1974
AT SASHA'S HOME

"The Leningrad battle lasted for close to three years. The enormous loss of life and the suffering the people had to endure…" I continue to read. Poom is the sound I hear as I close my papa's journal. Gently laying the journal down by my side, I lean up against the wall and close my eyes. I take deep breaths to help me relax myself, but my mind races wildly because of all I am reading. Reading about all the death and destruction completely overwhelms my senses. I sit there trying to take it all in.

Chirp, chirp, the beautiful sound of a bird's playful song rings happily in my ears. I get up from the floor and make my way over to the window. I have to crouch down so no one will see me. Outside, two blue jays are flying around each other. Their beautiful, bright blue feathers gleam in the sun. They fly away together and fly back, but this last time, they both fly away and only one comes back and sits on a higher branch. There is something sitting in the tree, but I cannot make it out clearly. Pain shoots through my back and knees from crouching for too long, so I sit on the floor under the window sill to get a better look. Little blue jays pop up from what appears to be a nest carefully resting up in a tree. High pitched excited chirps alert their mother that they are excited to see her. Their mother drops what looks like a worm into the nest and the three little blue jays are desperately clamoring to get some of it.

It is beautiful to watch nature in its most touching and honest moments, a mother taking care of her babies who are unable to fend for themselves. Their mother is making them strong so they can fly and be adept enough to fend for themselves out in the unknown of the cruel world. The sight brings me some peace, even if it is only temporary. Then, a thought occurs to me as I watch this interaction between parent and children. Perhaps this is what my papa was trying to do for me. By reading this, I can see the harsh realities of the world in spite of the sheltered life I have lived thus far.

While this beautiful sight is pleasant, thinking about my papa again upsets me. I carefully get up from the floor so as not to be seen and limp out the bedroom door to get a drink. With my toe throbbing from excruciating pain, I hobble down the hallway, but I stop when I hear Sasha's voice.

"Yes, here. What do you want me to do?" I peak out from behind the wall and see her speaking on the phone. She is playing nervously with her hair. She continually turns around, visibly paranoid about something. Her behavior is rather odd. I wonder who she is talking to. "Soon, I promise." She opens up a drawer and pulls out a piece of paper and pen. She scribbles something down while she listens intently on the phone. Suddenly, my throat becomes very scratchy. I try to quietly clear my throat, hoping the sensation will go away, but it gets worse. Whenever I try to cough, I catch it in my throat so no sound will come out and I can listen to what she is saying. My eyes fill with water as I battle the cough that wants to break free from the cage that is my throat. "Well then come..." Just like water from a flood gate being opened, my cough violently comes out. Sasha hangs up the phone quickly. "Taty?"

I limp out from behind the wall, as if I know nothing of a phone conversation. "My throat is bothering me. Can I please have a glass of water?"

She gives me an odd look. Scanning my face, she seems to be searching for an answer to the unspoken question of what I had heard. She nods her head and turns around. Reaching up, she opens a cabinet and takes out a clear glass. She turns on the faucet and holds the glass under the tap. The water quickly fills the glass up halfway. She pushes down on the handle to stop the beautiful flow of the crisp water and hands me the glass. She smiles at me. "Come on sit down." We pull out two chairs across from each other at her little kitchen table and gently sit down. I pick up the glass and put it up to my mouth. I try to drink it slowly and gently, but the coolness of the water is so soothing for my fiery throat. I begin to drink faster and with louder, more inviting gulps. When there isn't a drop left, I put the glass down and let out a loud and satisfying sigh. "Thirsty?" she asks, mischievously smiling at me.

"A little," I jokingly answer her.

"Did you finish reading your papa's journal?"

"Not yet."

"Find out anything interesting?"

"Death and destruction. Suffering, so much suffering, including my papa. He had a huge weight thrust upon his shoulders."

"The war?"

"Yes, the Great Patriotic War. When you hear great, you think of something beautiful and positive, but this war was far from that." I start thinking of what I have read. Then, I realize I am anxious to continue to see what happens. "I'm going to keep reading." I get up out of the chair and tuck it under the table.

"Taty, are you really sure you're up to this?" She puts her hand on my arm. Your papa just died and here you are reading about more death. Do you really think it's good for you?

"I'll be fine. I'm fine."

Sasha won't give up. "Why don't you give me the journal for now? I'll keep it safely hidden for you while you get some rest?" Have you looked at yourself in the mirror recently? You're so pale and have horrible dark rings under your eyes. You really don't look well."

I lash out, "Well, then, I guess I don't have a chance to win a beauty contest now, do I?" Sasha blanches. Instantly, I feel sorry for snapping at her. "I'm sorry. You're right, I am tired and sleep does sound wonderful. But I have to do this for Papa," I answer her.

"Please, give me the journal. It's for your own good. Give it to me."

"NO! If you won't let me read it here, I'll find another place to go."

Sasha looks dejected. She is visibly hurt by my snapping at her, but I am irritable from pain and exhaustion. "All right, Taty, all right." She puts a comforting hand to my shoulder. "I'm sorry. Do what you need to do. I won't argue with you anymore."

I shake my head up and down in accepting her apology. I limp back to her room to finish reading Papa's journal. I shut the door and sit back on the floor. Sitting there, I stare at the cover of Papa's journal once again. I have this uneasy feeling that I can't shake. Sasha seems too anxious to get her hands on Papa's journal and what about the phone conversation? Soon? What would be happening soon, something bad that she would see happen to me? I laugh and shake my head no. I am being crazy. She is probably talking to a friend about seeing her or him soon. A gentleman? Maybe she has a secret lover who she does not want to talk about with her best friend. That is probably it. "Be reasonable, Taty," I say to myself. This is Sasha I am thinking bad things about. She is practically a sister to me. She will not do anything to hurt me. I don't want to ask her about it directly, so as not to cause anymore hurt feelings. The stress of this enormous burden my papa has given me is probably making me unnecessarily paranoid.

I look up at the window. A person can easily look in there and discover me in here. Picking up her bed cover, I peer under Sasha's bed. There is more than enough room for me to fit under there. I pick up my papa's journal and crawl under the bed. My body is still throbbing from the pain it had endured earlier, but I try to ignore it. This task at hand is far more important. How can I complain about a few bruises when people suffered so much more agonizing pain during the war than I have? I slightly pick up the bed cover so enough light can shine on the page and make my reading easier. I lay flat on my stomach against the hard floor and put my feet up against the bottom of the bed so they won't stick out. The added pressure from my feet leaning up against the bed along with my stomach pressing down on the floor cause extreme discomfort for me. However, I am in a position where I am hidden and don't want to disrupt that. I take in a few breaths and exhale to try to make the discomfort more bearable. It seems to work, at least for the time being. Settling in, I open the journal and turn the pages until I find where I left off, continuing to read…

RALLYING THE TROOPS

While the battle over Leningrad continued to rage, the Germans in the south had advanced toward Stalingrad. Stalin was to send me to the front line to prepare an attack in the defense of Stalingrad on a future date in the month of November 1942. I knew how beleaguered everyone was from the length of fighting. Our morale was low. We all felt violated and we were losing our grip on the situation. One can have all the weapons, all the strategies, have full knowledge of the enemy, but if you do not have troops who believe in what they are fighting for, it would be very difficult to win a war of this magnitude.

Getting out of my car, I walked up to the camp site which consisted of numerous tents pitched on this very mountainous terrain. I walked past troops sitting and enjoying a meal. There was barely anything on their plates, but the few scraps of food were greatly appreciated for all the starving they had endured. They looked up as I walked by. Two men were watching me as I approached. They gave me a look as if they recognized me, but weren't sure if it was really who they thought I was or someone that bared an uncanny resemblance to that person.

"Is that Marshal Zhukov?" one of them whispered very loudly in the other's ear.

I turned to them and nodded my head in approval. Immediately, they stood up and saluted me causing their plates to be knocked off their laps and onto the ground. They bent down, desperately trying to pick up the food that dropped on the ground to salvage it for their consumption. While they blew away any dirt that covered the food, I walked over to them. Sharply they stood up and as they did, they hit each other's heads. They sat on the ground, trying to cope with the pain. One managed to get up from the ground without any other mishaps, but the other one tripped as he was getting up and once again knocked the food off his plate. He chose to leave it on the ground this time and just try to pick himself up without any other unfortunate incidents happening. Grimacing in pain while the two stood and saluted me, I looked sternly at them. Both were fearful I would reprimand them for their clumsiness. I examined them carefully. They were younger boys, barely older than myself when I first joined the military. As I looked closer at them, I realized they were twins! I laughed uncontrollably from this realization and what had just happened. Those poor boys didn't know whether to stand there perfectly still or join in the fun.

"You boys should start a comedy act and entertain our troops," I said through bouts of uncontrollable laughter. The boys both cracked a smile. "Just be careful with your food. You need your strength to fight," I said in a fatherly tone to them.

"Yes, sir." They answered at the same time.

I patted both of them on the back and shook their hands. I made my way up to the Headquarters tent, still laughing and shaking my head at the clumsy twins. They were rather endearing.

Inside the tent, two Commanders were talking and looking over papers. I stood there for a few moments, hoping they would acknowledge me. When they didn't, I cleared my throat. Immediately, they stood up.

"Marshal Zhukov, sir. We've been expecting you."

"Good. I'm glad you got word of my arrival."

One of the commanders grabbed a paper off his table. He walked it over and handed it to me. "We have the location--"

I interrupted him. "Before we get into details about the current operation, I want to meet with the men of this regiment, each one individually."

He seemed to be taken aback by my request, as if he'd never heard a person in my position ask something of this nature. "Ok, sir. I think we can get a few men in here so you can talk to them."

I shook my head in disagreement. "No, Commander. Not a few men. I want to meet with ALL the men in this regiment."

Now his face had a look of dismay written all over it, appearing to be very nervous. "But, sir, there are five hundred men in this division."

"Well, then, I guess I'm going to have to meet five hundred men day and night for the next few days. Won't I?" I shot back at him. He knew he had to obey my order, but at the same time probably thought I was crazy for making such a request. I knew what he was thinking. How could I spend my time with so many men on an individual basis before I do heavy planning for our attack? However, it was my obligation to instill in these men the fiery passion to fight again. I needed them to gain the fighting spirit back because it was going to be a long, hard battle and everyone's heart needed to be in it. At the same time, he appeared nervous, so I wanted to allay these fears that stirred within him due to my unusual request. "There's nothing to worry about, Commander. I simply want to talk to these men."

He shook his head in agreement, a look of calm poured over his face indicating he was no longer nervous. I sat myself at the table, debating in what position I should stay. I didn't want to appear too overbearing and make these men uncomfortable or nervous thinking they did something wrong. My goal was to get to know them on a more personal level. Yet, I couldn't be too comfortable and compromise my position of authority. I decided to sit leaned back against the chair, slightly crouching down. It would appear to them that it was a relaxed meeting, but yet I still displayed my full uniform with the medals I had won to show I was in charge and to garner respect.

The Commander brought the men in, one by one, to speak with me. It's amazing how many wonderful stories you can hear from complete strangers, although we all share the bonds of the military brotherhood. These men came from such diverse backgrounds and were of different ages. From teenage boys up to men almost as old as I was stood before me, and even though they looked physically dissimilar, they shared one similarity and that was that scared look in their eyes. It was a combination of the horror they experienced and meeting with me so informally.

Out of all the soldiers I had met, one encounter stuck in my mind. It was dusk, after we all had taken a break to eat. With my tea in hand to help keep me awake and powering full steam ahead like a locomotive, the commander sent in a man who had a very young face, but his particular build was that of a man in his later twenties. He was very tall and had thick brown hair that was very dirty and unkempt. His chocolate brown eyes curiously looked at me, anxiously waiting for a response from me.

"What is your name soldier?" I asked alleviating his anxiety.

"My name is Vadim Petrov, Marshal Zhukov."

I examined him again, trying to figure out how old he was but instead I wanted a straight answer. "How old are you, Vadim?"

"I'm twenty-three, Sir."

"Tell me about yourself."

He looked at me like a cloud just appeared in front of my face, shielding it from his view. He was taken aback by this assertion. "What would you like to know, Sir?"

"Anything you feel comfortable sharing with me." He and I looked into each other's eyes for a moment, trying to get a sense of where the other was coming from. It was apparent we were both curious about each other, but he was unsure of my motives. I was unsure of why he hesitated to tell me things about himself, but something told me that it was just nerves. He looked down at the floor, thinking of anything he could tell me. "I was married a year ago, and I have..." he struggled to get the words out. He swallowed hard, visibly upset. "I had an infant daughter. I, um... recently...lost them. Both my...wife and...daughter."

I could see the wall of tears build up in his eyes. He was struggling to fight them back to appear tough and thick skinned in front of me, but I could see how much he was suffering. I sat up in my chair and hunched over the desk, debating what I should say to him. I couldn't imagine what it was like to lose a child. A child isn't supposed to die before their parent. Being a parent is the most precious gift that could be bestowed upon someone. Raising a child and teaching them the ways of the world is a beautiful thing in its own right. Watching them grow from precious and innocent infants into the older and more mature man or woman and knowing you had an effect on the way they behave and view the world is a great honor and privilege. This poor, young man Vadim would never have that blessing bestowed upon him or have been able to utilize that privilege. Of course he could get married again and have more children, but I'm sure he would always wonder about the little infant daughter who was robbed of a full life ahead of her. "What happened to them?"

He tried to gain his composure to speak, but tears rolled gently down his cheeks. "I was off fighting and left them behind. Just…left them, new mother who gave birth not too long before, and I just…went off. They, um, were both…" He started to sob uncontrollably. Fighting with himself to muffle the sound of his sobbing, he continued on. "They…were…shot…by…the Germans." He quickly turned his back to me and buried his head in his hands. Muffled sobs echoed off of the palms of his hands.

I just sat there and watched him, completely frozen. It was hard not to run up to him and comfort him, but at the same time I needed to keep my position of authority from being compromised. As a papa, I understood how much pain he was in. I don't know how I would have reacted if something happened to my precious girl. So, I sat there in complete silence while Vadim composed himself. After a few minutes, he turned back around to me. His face was beet red and his eyes were swollen and matched the color of his face. He was sniffling to try and prevent anything from coming out of his nose. He wiped his nose on his sleeve. "I apologize, sir, for my emotional outburst. It was inappropriate of me."

This statement from him galvanized me from my chair and right in front of him. "Don't ever apologize to me over something like that. You have every right to be upset. Don't be brave in front of me, especially something concerning your family. I'm a papa, too. I know how difficult it is and I'm so sorry for your loss." He looked up at me with the saddest eyes, putting a dagger through my heart. All his emotional pain, angst, and guilt one could read in his eyes. "Please tell me what you're feeling," I begged him. I wanted to alleviate some of his pain by getting it off of his chest. I know it could never take the pain away fully by speaking about his feelings, but I felt it could ease him a little by opening up to someone who genuinely cared. "I should have stayed with them. I had to protect them and I failed. Because of me they're dead! Why couldn't it have been me instead? I would trade my life for theirs without any hesitation!" He burst out into tears again.

I put my arm around his shoulders to try and comfort him the best way I knew how. Vadim was more than half my age. I only knew him for mere minutes, but I felt very close to him. He felt like a son to me, a son who was suffering and needed his papa to comfort him and tell him it would be alright. I immediately flashed back to when I left home to join the military and was saying my good-byes to my papa. I wanted so much for him to show me a little affection as a parent who was genuinely worried for his child and wanted him to demonstrate to me how much I was loved. Perhaps my feeling of emptiness from my papa's send off for me was being filled by comforting Vadim and being like a papa figure for him. "Vadim, listen to me. You can't blame yourself for what happened. It's not your fault. You were doing what you were obligated to do and that's to fight, and that's what I need you to do now. I know you're hurt and you're suffering terribly, but we all are. You have to fight as difficult as it is. There's a reason why you were left here. We need all the strong, able bodies we can to carry on the war." I wanted to make sure no one was listening, so I went over to the tent flap to peek outside. The commander was standing just outside the tent, and I was certain he was in ear shot. I wanted to be able to speak openly and freely to Vadim. "Commander, go make the rounds about the camp and make sure everyone is ok."

He saluted me and walked away. I looked around once more, and when I was satisfied that all was clear; I went back inside to speak with Vadim. "We are in a dire situation now and are barely surviving. It's up to us now to get these barbarians off our land. No one is going to help us, no one. This is up to us, and we have the biggest responsibility resting on our shoulders. Despite all your pain, anger, and sadness and whatever other emotion you're feeling, I need you to give me your best effort. That's what's used to judge you as a man, how you handle adverse situations. So, I need you to be a man. Instead of channeling those feelings and using them to think of a way not to carry on, use them instead to stir yourself into action. Every time you grab your gun and aim it, think of your wife and daughter and don't hesitate to blow the enemy's brains out all over the ground for what they did to your family. For all the pain and suffering they caused all of us, never hesitate to poach one of those cowards. An eye for an eye."

He nodded his head in agreement, but seemed deeply confused about something. "Sir, you really don't think anyone will come to our aid."

"How? They're too busy fighting on the western front. It's every man for himself at a time like this or actually every country for itself. You can't expect anyone to fight your battles for you. We know our capabilities and we have to utilize them to the fullest, but we can't unless our men are fighting at their full strength. That's where you come in."

"Yes, I understand. I'll fight, sir."

I patted him on the back in an act of mutual understanding of what was expected from both of us. He was expected to take my command and fight to the death for the survival of our country. I had to plan out our attacks meticulously and make sure they were carried out down to the finest detail, but adjust our plans when necessary. I had to be a leader for these men. They were counting on me. "Go get a good night's rest. You'll need it."

"Thank you, sir."

He saluted me, and while he was saluting, I studied his face. I could see his manner was greatly improved from our man to man talk. He was still in obvious pain, but now he had a will and an ambition to carry on. He knew what he had to do. I felt like a proud papa of my son who was going to fight for his family's honor in the greatest battle. Vadim walked out of the tent and I sat back down at my table. This particular encounter took a great emotional toll on me. It reminded me how much I missed my family. Not just my wife and child, but also my sister. That little girl I had left all those years ago was now a full grown woman, a wife and mother to her own children. Like Vadim was robbed of watching his daughter grow up, I too felt robbed of watching my sister grow up. I hadn't heard much about her and she felt like a stranger to me in that regard. That place in my heart where she always was, felt particularly empty on that night. I prayed to God that she was still alive, and that her family was safe as well. If she was alive, I wondered what she was doing at that very moment. I hoped she had a roof over her head and some sort of food to eat, although food might as well have been like a rare diamond at that point in time, obscure. I wondered if she ever thought about me or if she was angry with me for "abandoning" the family. Maybe she didn't remember me at all. After all, she was only a little girl when I left. She never tried to get in contact with me, but I never expected her to. I'm sure mama told her that it wasn't possible for us to talk. Certain things about me couldn't be discovered, and they would be discovered if they found out exactly who my family was.

It became do or die in late 1942. The Germans would be pushing their frontlines closer to our heart of Moscow through Kursk. Moscow was standing and waiting for what appeared to be the inevitable destruction. Stalin wanted to order a major, offensive attack against the enemy, but I knew this would spell the end for us.

After speaking with my troops, I had a meeting with Stalin. At that time, I went in there with the attitude that he was going to listen to what I wanted to do and what needed to be done. The situation was grim, but I had a plan I thought would be successful. I marched into his office with a newly found confidence. Motivating my troops was a big accomplishment for me. I felt I had them ready to fight, but I needed Stalin's approval to carry out my plan. With map in hand, I spread it on his desk right on top of what he was working on.

"What the hell do you think you're doing?" he snapped at me.

"Premiere Stalin, we need to discuss how we should proceed next."

"The only thing I want to hear from you is that you carried out my orders."

He was agitating me greatly with his stubbornness, but I was determined to match him in that adamance. I had to appease him by incorporating his plan into mine. Operation manipulation was under way. "Winter," I said and stopped without saying anything else.

"Well? What about it?"

"That's the goal we share with the Germans is winter."

"Why are you wasting my time with this nonsense?" he snarled at me.

I ignored him and continued. "Hitler wants to have us beaten before the winter comes. His armies won't be able to handle the upcoming, harsh Soviet winter. They don't have enough supplies, enough manpower, and their weapons aren't designed to withstand the brutality I feel this coming winter will bring." I could tell I was losing Stalin, so now came the part of appeasing him. "I couldn't agree more with you, Premier Stalin, that we need to launch a major offensive against Hitler's army, but we have to prolong the skirmishes and wait until this prolonging forces the Germans to wander right into our winter trap." I stalled to study Stalin's reaction.

Stalin glanced up at me. The anger was melting away from him like the snow did after fighting through the coming winter, leaving the Germans weak and depleted before we would launch our major, offensive attack in the spring. "Go on, I'm listening."

"They're using all their might on us now; using everything they can to annihilate us. We have to battle with enough men to hold them off until the winter comes in." I put my index finger on an area north of Moscow. "Factories are here, a large number of them. Right now, they are producing items that are not needed at a time like this. We need to convert them into weapon-producing powerhouses, manufacturing artillery, tanks, and everything that we need. From this point, we have to feed the weapons through Moscow and to the frontlines. Additional troops have to be sent in with the new equipment that is being produced." Stalin started to become his unyielding self, instead of being intrigued.

"It's impossible," Stalin asserted.

"It's very possible and we have to. At the rate they can manufacture our other goods; they can do the same for whatever weapons we want." He was stone faced, teetering on the fence of whether to trust me. So, I went in for the kill. "I want to build a major blockade around Moscow, using everyone who is able to work and have them build the different traps to be set up. I am willing to supervise all this activity, and if anything goes wrong with my plan, I'm willing to suffer the consequences. I know it will work and you have to trust me."

Stalin stared at me, still stone faced. What he said next was what I needed to hear. "Do what you must," Stalin said.

Do what you must, I thought. Yes, I was now doing what I must. Our strong population was going to be put to work to fight off these dangerous invaders. Sending out a widespread proclamation, I requested all healthy and sane women and older children to work at our factories. They would gather outside the doors, waiting to be let into their new life's purpose. No longer would they solely care for their children, feeding them and washing them. Now, they would take the place of their husbands who were the man power for these weapons they were producing. Instead of baking bread, their hands would be used to mold different pieces into one weapon that will be a killing machine. I would bet that a vast majority of these women had never seen a tank or gun up close before they started working in these factories. All this was cast aside for the greater good, our survival.

As the air grew more frigid, it reminded us that our deadline was quickly approaching for both sides. The German foot soldiers and tanks rolled in, continuing to push the front lines in on Moscow. Our anti-tank guns were set up and shooting off at every opportunity to blast a tank to tiny, unrecognizable pieces. Our foot soldiers were in a shoot out with the enemy. Back and forth the firing of the bullets continued, spraying each other's bodies with the small killers that were unleashed from the guns. By January 1943 my men and I were victorious in this Battle of Stalingrad with the winter proving as I had told Stalin to be of great assistance; however, other battles between my army and Hitler's forces continued to rage.

The back and forth fighting persisted until the Germans unleashed their major weapons. The tanks the Germans used before were smaller and more manageable to fight against, but these new tanks were called Tiger tanks. The name described these tanks perfectly as the predators they were. The camouflaged colors of their armor were used to conceal themselves perfectly before they would unleash their powerful artillery fire from the most powerful weapon in the world at that time. Our anti-tank artillery fire was no match. It would shoot free from the gun and the missiles would merely bounce off the armor of the Tiger tanks. Nothing could pierce through to the heart of those monsters. With artillery shells bouncing off, the Tiger tanks pushed through with great ease. The tanks would roll slowly into a crowd of our foot soldiers. The soldiers would watch in horror as the giant Tigers would pounce on them and crush them under their chained wheels. All you could hear were the blood curdling screams and crunching of their bones as the Tigers would have their way with these soldiers. The others would run away, trying to salvage their lives. The German foot soldiers would walk right next to these Tigers and shoot the ones who weren't crushed to death.

I remember standing on the horizon with my binoculars watching as thousands of men were running in the opposite direction and the Germans were marching forward with ease. We needed our soldiers to hold the Germans at this place to allow for the feeding in of new weapons and soldiers. I rode up near to the front on my horse. The cool, spring air stung into my face, continuing to serve as a reminder of our fate's ticking clock. Atop my horse, I galloped around the soldiers running away like a madmen.

"What the hell are you doing? Get back in there!" I yelled. Some heeded what I said seriously and went back and fired their guns at the enemy. Most of them continued running away. After all, they probably thought, they would rather face my angry yelling than withstand being crushed by one of those monsters. I was so angry; I jumped off my horse, actively seeking someone who could help me with my plan. I found a soldier who was standing tall and proud at the front line, aiming his gun at an enemy soldier and firing off. I watched as each one he aimed at fell to the ground. This is a warrior, I had thought to myself. He's perfect. I went in and grabbed him from behind. With bullets being sprayed wildly, I pulled him behind my horse so the animal could shield us from any stray bullets. "I need you to find chains for me and whoever is running away is going to be chained to our stationary artillery guns!"

The soldier ran off and gathered numerous other soldiers to help carry out this task. They found the large chains and grabbed these men one by one who were running off. I joined in the action and grabbed a hold of one soldier. "Get back in there and fight like a man!" I yelled at him. I could see the fear in his eyes and felt as tremors went through his body.

"No, I can't. Those things…those things," he kept saying.

"Then, you'll be treated like a coward!" I dragged him by his shirt and found a chain. With him in my hand, I pushed him up against one of the artillery guns. Quickly, I wrapped the chain around the gun, round and round. I attached the ends underneath a post on the gun. The only things I kept free were the soldier's arms; otherwise the rest of his body was chained to that gun so he couldn't run away. "Shoot at the enemy or I will shoot you at a public gathering!"

He fed the artillery shells into the gun as fast as he could, and was shooting wildly at the enemy. He was clearly frustrated he wasn't free to move and had no choice but to do as I ordered him.

Two of our soldiers were chained to each gun. Some had been blown up by the fire of the tanks and some had been set on fire, appearing to be like a pig being roasted on an open fire. However, most of them were doing their job and killing off the German foot soldiers. The Tiger tanks, however, kept rolling towards their destination of Moscow.

My next mission was to organize the traps. I gathered thousands of women who weren't working in the factories. Their job was to dig deep trenches to trap these vicious Tiger tanks. We didn't have the weapon capability to defeat them, so we were going to do it the old fashioned way. These women dug with all their energy, time not on our side. The Tiger tanks were rolling toward the heart of our country at an alarming rate. These women, shovels in hand, wildly pierced into the earth, tossing the dirt in all directions without a care in the world where it landed. Sometimes, the dirty earth would land on them. They would never flinch. The air grew warmer and helped soften the ground. Digging and more digging would take place. The Tiger tanks were rolling over the earth, driven on getting to the heart of our Motherland as fast as they could. They were determined to finish us off soon. More of the furious digging against the rolling of the Tiger tanks continued through all sorts of weather conditions.

Then, there they were. The vicious predators were now in front of us. It was right in Kursk on this July 1943 when we were about to engage in the largest tank battle the world had ever seen. Now was the test to see if we would survive.

I had placed our soldiers behind the ditches, perfectly setting the trap and luring the enemy in. Our soldiers just stood in place and fired as the Tiger tanks drew closer. With the tanks pushing forward, you could almost see the gleeful anticipation in their moves, showing that they were confident they were going to succeed in quickly annihilating us. Our soldiers stood there, frozen in fear of these monsters. The Tiger tanks were now lunging forward to crush us, when instead of pushing forward, a sudden and disguised rise of dirt just at the mouth of the trench jerked the tanks upward. They tried to push the tanks forward, but with no luck. We watched as these Tiger tanks rolled over the rise and fell down into the trenches, making it impossible to move either forward or backward. They were stuck in this disabling position with confusion as to what had just happened to them. They fired their guns off to try and get free, but their shots would just penetrate the ground and not serve to free them. If they shot through a particularly hard part of the ground, the shell would bounce back and blow up the tank from its own fire.

Our soldiers trudged through the trenches and now our vicious assault began. Our soldiers broke into these tanks through the hatch on the top, and fired their guns into the safe stations of the Tiger tanks, killing the brains and operators of these monsters. The blood would splat up from the holes, fueling my men to jump up on these tanks like monkeys swinging from tree to tree and finishing these things off for good. According to plan, since they were stalled right where we wanted them, we fed our new weapons and men into the action. Now, the positions of David and Goliath were switched. This battle of Kursk cost Hitler so greatly that it made it impossible for the German Army to ever again match my Soviet Army equally or supersede it.

Before long, the wrath of another winter in 1943 was unleashed upon our Soviet soil. We continued fighting knowing that Hitler's aim was to make our Soviet people extinct through mass murder by starvation and exposure to the harsh winter. Some Soviet civilians and prisoners of war managed to inch their way back behind our front lines, barely escaping the blood thirsty Germans. As they walked to safety, they appeared as walking skeletons after being stripped of all their winter clothes and left to die from exposure in the snow. These walking skeletons seemed to have risen from the grave, intent on their mission to come back to our welcoming arms.

The winter wreaked vengeance on the Nazis as if punishing them for using the Soviet winter for help in their elimination of our own civilians and prisoners of war.

Without being able to advance, the Germans ran low on supplies as I had predicted. Trying desperately to keep warm with the clothes they had, they would build massive fires that would sometimes result in the need for them to use some of their vital weapons to feed the fires. The air was so frigid, if your bare skin ever touched it, it would feel like it was burning right off of you. Their stomachs were violent from their emptiness because of the lack of food. Frozen German corpses littered the snow, as the needling cold and the emptiness of their stomachs won the battle over their bodies. Some Germans would shoot their horses in cold blood, ripping their fresh, chunky meat from the bones to place on the open fire to cook and eat. Desperate to dig their teeth into the scrumptious flesh to fill the emptiness and appease the growling, it still didn't save them from their violent deaths.

Consumed with intense anger and passionate hatred, we pushed the front lines further west. My offensive attacks in Operation Bagration were a continuing success. No longer were the Germans fighting to pierce through our heart and capture Moscow. Instead, they were fighting for their survival. I ordered border patrols to be set up along all our borders, so the allies of the Germans could not feed more men, weapons, and other necessities. Without the supplies to help fuel the Germans voracious power, they were left alone on our soil to fight a losing battle.

Like fearless warriors, we pounded them with all our force. They dropped like flies all around us. Summer would be turning into fall and any coolness reminded them of the atrocious bitterness of our winters. With one last final effort, they battled back and regained some of the fierceness they once possessed. They shot at us with whatever weapons they had. However, the few, vital weapons they had were put to good use. The memories of the previous winter apparently came back to them. Not wanting to face Mother Nature's wrath once again, they felt that our wrath was a more viable alternative.

As the strength of the Germans slightly increased, ours matched theirs ten fold. We rolled out our own tanks now to help finish the job. Riding in from the north, east, and south to surround them and force them back was our strategy. It didn't save our foot soldiers, though. They were no match for the enemy soldiers. Their guns wildly pierced through our men, desperate to carry out Hitler's mission and go home before the bitter cold could reach their bones. Rolling over the terrain, our tanks came to the rescue of our men. Thousands of our heavy KV and T-34 medium tanks, with the only thing on the minds of their drivers, were to fire their angry shells into the flesh of the Germans. We were now the predators, hunting our prey on the ground and rolling over their helpless bodies, inspired by the slogans on our tanks which read, "Victory Will Be Ours!" From the north and south, came the firing of our reserve armored divisions. Smoke and burning flesh filled the air, and the tanks from the east plowed through the Germans like they were little insects being crushed under a human's foot. Back they went, far back before we could inflict them with more casualties. Our power and ability to instill fear in the enemy now matched Mother Nature's.

The dark cloud had been lifted from over our Motherland. We had already pushed the Germans back to the border of Poland. Now we were launching a full out strike against them. It wasn't enough to extract them from our land. We had to finish them off in the most aggressive way we could. With my men, we were going to charge mercilessly through Poland. We marched with such great force and energy because of the tremendous victory we had achieved. There was a new sense of pride amongst us, and it was refreshing to see. Instead of being the helpless victims, we were now the attackers. We were desperate to seek vengeance. Now, we wanted to taste the blood of the Germans. It was their turn to experience the rash of our anger and hostility toward them. With this thought, we tracked on into Poland, hoping to kill as many of those savages as we could. The demon that was trying to possess us was being exorcised back to the depths of hell. What we encountered in our pursuit was enough to shock one's nervous system.

We had received a report in July 1944 about some type of camp called Majdanek that was located in Lublin, Poland. Many of our prisoners of war had been sent there, and we were on a quest to free them. We also knew of something else that was going on there. These camps were a façade of a labor camp when in reality they were a place of death and a killing machine. I had heard stories about their methods, mainly gas chambers. It's one thing to hear about something. It could be rumors or speculation after all. However, seeing it in person with your own eyes is too unbelievable. What I encountered left an impression on me that has remained with me for the rest of my life from that point forward.

On that July day in 1944, my group of fifty soldiers and I were walking through fields of grass. There was beautiful, green grass as far as the eye could see. The sun was shining its bright and warm rays down on us, and the sky was a beautiful, blue hue. We kept walking further ahead, our legs starting to grow tired from the distance we had traveled. I was breathing in the fresh air when suddenly a stench hit me hard in the face. I breathed in deeper, trying to take in more air to decipher what exactly that smell was. It was a burning smell like someone had put a meal to heat in an oven and left it in there far over the time it was due to come out.

Out in the distance, we saw numerous buildings and a large tower. There was something that surrounded the perimeter of this area of buildings. As we moved closer, the long, enrapturing, barbed wire came into clearer focus. There was a crowd of men who stood perfectly still, watching us as we came closer. The burning smell consumed my lungs. I kept coughing, trying to catch my breath as we stood. When moving closer, I realized the smell was much worse than that of burnt food. It was burning flesh. It smelled like someone set a group of people ablaze and their skin mixed with the fiery aroma of hell.

When we reached the gate, the sight caused me to stop dead in my tracks. A somber grayness hung over this camp and not anywhere else. It was such a shocking contrast with the blue sky. It wasn't caused by anything physical, like a storm moving in with its ominous clouds. It seemed to permeate from the horror and destruction that was caused here. Seeing these men was a horror unlike anything I had experienced before. I had watched men blown up in front of my eyes, but what stood in front of me now was a far worse sight. Emaciated, skeleton-like men stood watching us with looks of curiosity and distrust. They seemed like caged animals standing behind the barbed wire, just there to be on display for their shocking appearance. Their bones stuck out everywhere and their human form was merely a skeleton covered by their thin, dried out skin. If they had anything to eat, you could probably see it in resting in their stomachs. That's how small and transparent their stomachs appeared.

Very slowly, I made my way up to the opening in the fence. One man stood in front of all the others, as they pushed themselves back further behind him. You could see the fear in their hollowed faces and dark-ringed eyes as I made my way in. My soldiers tried to follow me in, but I held them back so we would not overwhelm these prisoners. The man and I stood facing one another. This was by far the most bizarre encounter I had ever experienced with another human being. "I'm Marshal Zhukov. We're here to set you free." I might as well have spoken in some ancient language that hadn't been spoken in years because all of them just stood there from what appeared to be confusion. Waiting for a response from them, my annoyance took over. "I said you are free to go! Leave!"

The man moved closer to me and glared. The anger from deep within him permeated through his eyes. "What do you expect us to do? Cheer wildly and throw ourselves on the ground at your feet?

His scathing remarks took me by surprise. Normally, if someone spoke to me like this, I would scold him with harsh language and remand him to a lower status. However, this man was such a pitiful sight, I felt sorry for him. Actually, it wasn't so much the sight of him that made me pity him, but the way he said his remark. It was meant to sting and insult me, but it had absolutely no affect on me. The way it came out was a complete lack of emotion in those words, like his ability to feel anything was completely gone from his soul. He wasn't able to feel happiness, sadness, anger, or hate anymore, as if it had been completely sucked out of him and would never return. "Can you show me around?" I cautiously asked him.

"Do I have much of a choice?" he asked in that same tone, one that was meant to be scathing but came out as nothing more than a question.

I turned back to my men to address them. "Take care of these prisoners. Give them food and water. Help get them out of here." Upon my orders, my men sprung into action to aide. My attention focused again on my guide and he proceeded ahead of me. He was hobbling from one leg to the other. My eyes proceeded downward and I was shocked to see he was missing his right foot! I had seen things like this before, but suddenly noticing it is what surprised me. "Uh...what happened to you?" I asked him.

He stopped dead in his tracks and turned while leaning on his left foot and hobbling around with the stump. He saw I was staring at his missing appendage.

"I had an infection in the ball of my foot that was slowing me down in my work. So, I went to the doctor to get medicine for it and instead he took a giant carving knife and sliced it through my ankle. He couldn't cut through my bone with it. So he left me lying there until he got a saw to cut through my bone. That's how my infection was cured."

"A doctor did that to you?" I was stunned by this.

"You heard me, a doctor." He turned back around and continued to hobble along.

His account of what happened to his foot rang in my ears again as we walked to our first destination. His words were so hollow, like his face that was deprived of any fat on it. I imagined his account in my mind. Since his words didn't allow me to feel the reality of his horrible account, I decided to put myself in his place. I pictured myself working on a laborious task out in the field, when suddenly my foot had terrible pains shooting through it. Walking up to tell one of those Nazi savages, he grabbed my arm with all the hatred he felt for me in his grip around my forearm. He dragged me to the clinic nearby. Sitting there on the table, the doctor walked into the room. His white lab coat was a welcoming sight. That sight reminded me of how I was going to be alleviated of these sharp pains. The doctor took my foot in a firm grasp and looked at it for a few moments. Then, his eyes looked at me. Instead of the warmth, caring, and compassion a doctor normally shows his sick and helpless patient to ease their mind, his eyes were cold, callous, and filled with such hatred. With a flash, there it was that swastika arm band. It's the saw that cuts through your soul. Now, it was cutting through the flesh of my ankle. Those sharp teeth were eating away at my flesh. Every time I screamed out in pain, the doctor dug deeper in, as if the agony he was causing me gave him unbridled and passionate pleasure. I grabbed a towel that was near me and bit down into it to muffle my screams, hoping the doctor would stop the cutting. However, he kept digging deeper and deeper into my flesh until he hits the hard bone. Needles were shooting through my leg, traveling up from my ankle where the deep cut was bleeding me dry. I drifted in and out of consciousness while the doctor grabs his saw that would dig its jagged edges straight through my bone until the stubborn appendage was cut free from my leg. The doctor rubbed the blade with his coat to shine it up and then slowly guided it down toward the bone as I drifted out of consciousness...

"Our first stop," my guide interrupted my daydream.

I shook my head to better focus myself on what I would encounter. I looked back to see what we had passed and what I had missed while my thoughts wandered to another place and time. Numerous, ominous appearing buildings that looked out at the long, enrapturing barbed wire helped to keep me in like the other animals. I turned back around to the building that stood in front of us. We were in front of a wooden door with a small little hole near the top. It matched the rest of the building, which looked like a converted horse barn. The man tried to pull the door open, but the heaviness of it was too much for his weak and tattered body. I quickly walked up behind him. It took my whole stocky body to push open that door. I took a moment to catch my breath from the exertion. Before I made my way inside, something on the wall caught my eye. A sign that said "Bad und Desinfektion" hung proudly. Since it was in German, I needed help deciphering its meaning. "What does that mean?" I called out to question the man who had already ventured inside.

He hobbled back out to see what I was talking about. While staring at the sign he answered, "Bath and disinfection. They thought they were going in for a hot shower after a long day of work, only to come out as corpses who were going to be put into the crematorium."

He turned around and hobbled back into the room. I managed to tear my eyes away from the sign and followed him in. This room was a massive size. It could easily fit four hundred people packed in together. There was a single pipe that ran along the wall. Aside from that, the room was bare except for the window that was located up by the ceiling. It was so high that no one could see through it, like it served as a reminder of the beautiful outside world these people would forever be deprived of. Looking around, the bare white walls were splattered with blue stains. I walked up to one that was near the window to closely examine it. I immediately recognized what it was upon closer examination. It was the gas Cyclon B, used primarily as an insecticide. Even with my reading of Hitler's true feelings in his books, it had never really sunk into me just how much hatred he had for the Jews. It wasn't until I saw this sight that the realization hit me. Releasing insecticide into a large group of innocent human beings was the lowest act any human being could do to another. These people were killed like they were annoying flies buzzing around your ear. It's one thing when you are fighting a battle and need to use any measure necessary to destroy your enemy, but to corral innocent humans into a room just to fill their lungs with poison and watch them drop like the pests they were thought of is something no human should ever do. The only way to explain this horrendous act was to describe it as not of this world. It was something evil that lurked deep beneath our feet in the fiery pit of hell.

Walking around the perimeter of the room examining the blue stains, I found a door along the back wall and cautiously opened it. Inside, were numerous canisters. There were a pile of empty ones thrown in the corner of the room. What shocked me was how many unused cans were neatly stacked up against the wall, just waiting to consume more victims.

There was a piece of wood by the unused cans that appeared to be blocking something. I stealthily stepped through cans and other junk on the floor in pursuit of seeing what the wood was concealing from my view. I had to move some things out of the way. One of them I picked up to discover it was a gas mask. Those murderers spared themselves the insecticide poisoning that ravaged their victims. Finally reaching the wood, I pried it open to find a large hole. I looked through it and had a clear view of every angle in the room. So that was why the gas mask was by the hole. They put it on and watched their pests die a slow and painful death. Those poor people were probably clawing at the walls and begging with their executioners to set them free, but silence answered them back.

I went back out into the room where the man was staring up at the window. I moved closer to him so I could see his face. His eyes had a far away look in them as if he was caught in a distant memory. "When I was working in the fields, I used to hear the terrible screams coming from in here. They were such horrible screams," he said to me. "Such panicked screams. They used to try to drown it out with the loud motors by the building. But once you hear those sounds, they stay right there in your ears. You never forget those sounds." His eyes winced, and this was the first sign of emotion he showed. It was like my presence reminded him what it was like to be human again and have the emotions that humans do.

"You know, I never got your name."

"It was Daniel Rosenberg, but what does that matter anymore."

"Was?" I questioned him from this strange statement of him referring to himself in the past.

"I can honestly say I died the moment I walked through that gate. They might as well have put me in here with the rest of them. I don't know why they didn't and I'm still here." He looked around at the room and seemed to silently honor his fellow man that perished within these walls. "Let's move on." He hobbled back outside and I followed like an obedient dog behind him. As we drew closer to a smoke stacked building that was half destroyed from what looked like someone trying to burn it down, the smell of the burning flesh pierced through my nose again. Instead of letting Daniel try to open the door, I immediately went for it. I swung it wide open and let him hobble in ahead of me. Inside was one enormous large room. Ovens were lined up side by side along the walls. The heat from them was still trapped in the atmosphere, wanting to escape but was forced to be confined in this room. I sauntered over to one of the ovens while scanning what was left of the room. The brick ovens stood ominously with its doors flung open. I looked inside the nearest one. Ashes lay near the open doors, a reminder of what happened in here when the doors were shut. I looked up through the opening in the roof. The grayness still loomed over the area, like heaven was in mourning for these victims. Daniel was standing at an oven directly across from mine, just staring directly into the opening. I proceeded towards him very slowly so I wouldn't disturb him. He was so deep in thought that he was completely frozen in place. I peered into the open door and laying there were full skeletal remains. In looking at it, my mind kept going over how these people had the right to have the remains treated after death taken away from them. When one is an average person, they can choose if they want to be buried or cremated. Of course, once someone is dead, he or she may not get was requested. At least the person dies thinking their own body will be discarded as he or she wishes by someone who cares. You have no choice in how you die, that of course being left to God. At least you get a choice of a proper burial or cremation. How was I supposed to know what the person in the oven over there wanted to do? Maybe he had a family plot in some beautiful cemetery where he could spend eternity with those he held close to his heart. Instead these demons robbed him of this opportunity and left him in a cooking oven so they could satisfy their insatiable appetite for torturing their victims. This poor man was now trapped here to spend his eternity wandering these grounds in search of those he loved, only to be alone.

"I wonder who that was," Daniel questioned out loud, but was really asking himself this question?

Out of thin air, a thought came to me. They tried to burn down this place, but apparently didn't have time. I was sure they would try to destroy the other camps before we could get there. This elaborate showcase that the Germans built no longer served its purpose, so those cowards wanted the evidence destroyed, and all the torture they inflicted upon innocent people would then go unpunished. I couldn't let that happen. I would not allow all these people to have died in vain. Their story would be told.

"Come on," I ordered to him, as he just stood, muttering something under his breath. "What are you doing?" I asked him.

"I'm saying a Kaddish prayer for this person."

"It is wonderful that I see you still believe in Judaism, even after everything that has been done to you. Somehow, the Jews are always considered a problem to people. Someone hears you are a Jew and you're limited in what you can do in life. They don't even bother with you once they hear you are a Jew."

"Faith is all I have left. Tell me something, Marshal Zhukov. Do you hate Jews?"

"Not at all. I actually...I need to get back to my men." I didn't want to talk about the subject anymore.

We made our way back to the entrance. I walked over to a soldier. "I want you to take the camera and go through all these buildings and capture completely what went on here," I ordered. "People will deny this horror ever happened and I want proof that they can't refute. The soldier saluted and went on his way. "Can you show me where you slept?" I asked Daniel. He nodded and hobbled ahead, showing me I should follow.

We slowly went along until we reached the outside of a wooden building. The door was already open. We stepped inside to a bare, cold room that housed a line of bunks on either side.

"Well, this is where your tour ends. I can't be in here anymore." I watched him start to hobble out before he turned around. "Thank you for finally rescuing us," he said and hobbled back out.

He tried to be appreciative, but his statement really hit me again with how devoid of emotion it sounded. I walked around looking through all the bunks. I imagined all the people who were stuffed into these bunks, deprived of even the basic comfort of having your own personal space to sleep in. Even if you were forced to sleep on the floor, at least you had space to move around without someone crunched right on top of you. I walked down through the room, scanning carefully. When I reached the opposite end of the room, something caught my eye. A pile of striped clothing was stuffed into the corner. I reached down and picked it up. The stench of body odor was extremely overwhelming, as I laid out the wrinkled clothes. When I was fanning them out, something yellow glided gently into the air and lay to rest on the floor about a foot away from me. My eyes fixated on the yellow object, and as I grew closer, I saw that it was a Star of David. I picked it up and sat down on the nearest part of the lower bunk. Shining on the Star in black, bold print was the word "JUDE". I hadn't noticed it on the other clothes, and this Star appeared to be ripped off from somewhere else. This person seemed to want to cling to this object of their religion very carefully. Daniel was right when he said that all they had was their faith.

Like a flood, all the emotions I was trying to keep bottled up inside of me, rushed their way to the surface. Thinking about the evidence of destruction and suffering I saw and then this talk of faith made tears well up in my eyes. I had never cried in my life before this, because as a proud man and leader of the army, I had to keep my emotions out of the equation.

Daniel's last words to me rang in my ears, especially the word "finally". Yes, finally. If my army and I had gotten there sooner, we could have saved more people. If only Stalin listened to not just me but the warnings about Hitler sooner, so much suffering could have been spared. If only that monster, Hitler, could have been stopped long before. Why couldn't anyone stop him until now? Why did people judge others because of their nationality and religion? As the warm tears slowly rolled down my cheeks, I

STORMING OF BERLIN

There I was the warrior again in the spring of 1945, but now my sword was swiftly piercing toward the monster's heart, and it involved finishing off Hitler and his Party in Berlin. My army and I had been heading to the west for months, plowing through to get here to the German border. Everything Hitler thought he had in his grasp was now ours. Like mad men, we stormed through Poland and Prussia, all the way into Hungary and every other territory they had thought was theirs. The sword plunged deeper and deeper as we traveled in trucks to the final showdown in hell. We were all happy and proud of what we had accomplished and how we fought this monster. However, we were also physically and emotionally drained from everything we had experienced.

We meandered up and down, winding through the mountain roads. As we did, it seemed to represent our journey through this terrible war. When we headed down from the top, it was like in the beginning of the war, when we were spiraling out of control- completely unprepared, physically outmatched, facing indescribable destruction, and having very little capabilities to defend ourselves. Every time we went up a mountain, it felt exhilarating and full of promise, almost like we were making progress and pushing forward. Now, it felt as if we were the ones who held all the cards and control over the Germans. They were now the ones barely hanging on, in desperate need of the help. As we proceeded closer to Berlin, anxiety continued to build up. When the Germans invaded our land and the land of others, they had come with the strength in years of preparation. My army and I were now the conquering invaders and we needed to make sure we overtook them quickly before they could reorganize themselves and powerfully fight us back. It was a race against time once again.

As I looked back at the men in the truck, you could see the exhaustion written on their faces. Their eyes had deep, dark rings under them. Like counting the rings of a tree to determine its age, you could count the rings under their eyes to determine their level of distress and exhaustion. These men had gone through so much, fought a relentless enemy and many of them lost family members in the process. Not only lost them, but they perished in the most horrible, unfathomable way that no rational human could ever conceive. This type of loss extended beyond their family members as well. Going through the camp was such a shock, that it really made you question how something so horrible could have been real. That's why I was so glad we had documentation of all that because, like is said, a picture is worth a thousand words.

The trucks finally came to a halt at a destination point I had assigned. Slowly, the men filed out with weapons in hand. Some of them had been stirred to a fully awake state by the sudden stop while others were so prepared to destroy the enemy, you could read it in their eyes even past those horrible dark rings. I watched them all file into a straight line up against the horizon in the background. I needed each and every single one of these men to have the same fighting spirit, which is why I chose to travel on this leg of the journey with them.

I stepped out of the truck, and immediately they all came to attention and saluted. Step by step with my hands behind my back, I examined each and every one of the men standing before me. While they were looking ahead, I could tell out of the corner of their eyes that they were looking to see if my body language could give them clues as to why I had gathered them there. I just kept a completely neutral face, while walking up and down in front of them. When I felt fully comfortable with my thorough examination and all of them had their attention focused on me, I proceeded into my speech. "I've gathered you here today in order for all of you to understand the great feat that is ahead of each and every one of us. This war has been long and extremely difficult. Many Soviet lives have been lost. Most of you have lost someone close to you. Some of you have even lost children." I remember stopping in front of Vadim to see his reaction. He stood perfectly still, but looked at me. I smiled at him in an understanding, sympathetic fashion. The corner of his mouth curled up in a half smile, to reciprocate my warm greeting to him while not flinching from his position that acknowledged my authority.

"From today, and for however long it may take to defeat Hitler, we must keep fighting hard, no matter what the cost. The way we fought to defend our beloved Moscow, with fervent passion, that is how they will fight to defend Berlin, their very own heart and soul. Just when you think you are too tired and there has been enough bloodshed, you think of all our people who starved to death or were brutalized by these savages. Fight in memory of all our people who were lost. They came on our land, destroyed our homes, and killed innocent people all in an effort to take over our great country of the Soviet Union. This enemy shows no remorse for its actions. It's up to all of you to make them remorseful. I'm warning you now, if I see any of you running in fear from the enemy, the consequences will be severe. I'll forcefully strap you to a field artillery gun, like I've done in the past if that's what it takes for you to fight."

Now, they all appeared ready to fight with fire in their eyes and desire in their hearts, stemming from vengeance. We were ready to surge through full force. That giant wave of water Hitler wanted to use to drown us was now going to be used against him, except it wasn't going to be water. It was going to be a wave of angry, forceful Soviet soldiers coming to demolish everything in their paths and drown the Germans with all their fury. "Get ready to deploy men!" I ordered

"Sir, yes sir!" everyone shouted and marched off in an organized fashion to prepare for their efforts.

Looking out over the horizon, I was still concerned. This was our biggest mission on foreign soil. We never had to conquer a foreign city as large as Berlin. If we failed in our mission, Hitler's power would rise again. He had to be finished once and for all.

"It should overwhelm you. You'll never get this glorious city!" a familiar and angry voice boomed behind me. However, it wasn't the same forceful, seething, evil tone it once was. The angry tone was a façade for the desperation and worries that really consumed him.

Slowly, I turned around and there stood the monster Hitler in one of my visions once again. I was shocked at just how much his appearance had changed. He was a shell of his former self. No longer could he inspire fear with his evil aura; now, he looked old and weathered from the sweeping defeats we had sprung upon him and from the crashing blow of reality that had been bestowed upon him over the last two years. No longer would he be the most admired leader of his glorious empire, using innocent people as circus freaks in his meticulously laid out museums that everyone would visit after his master, Aryan race overtook the world's population. He tried desperately to cling onto this image, but I could easily see right past it. This gave me a renewed hope that we would go in there and crush him.

Now, I turned to my vision of Hitler and said, "We are going to take Berlin with every fiber of our bodies and weapons. We are going to unleash an all out offensive attack on you- bombard you with artillery attacks, tanks, fighter planes, and every possible way we can and surround you from all directions. Let you feel there is no escape from impending defeat. There will be no way out for you, and you'll surrender unconditionally and look us in the eyes and face the pain and suffering we have felt."

"Never! You'll have to kill us all!" the vision of Hitler said.

"Then so be it!" I shouted at the vision.

After that challenge, he quickly evaporated into thin air. You could still feel his lingering presence, especially the spot where he had been. Right now though, my focus was on getting all of our men and weapons prepared for the start of the battle. The bomber planes were waiting off in the distance, like cougars waiting to pounce on their prey. The rocket launchers were really poised and ready. I remember examining them when they came out of the factory. They carried four missiles in each of the holders. Instead of just firing one sharp piercing shot to cause immense destruction, multiply that by four. Being there in the pit of hell, forced me to think as evil did. I imagined those missiles launching in their clockwise fashion quickly one by one and mercilessly destroying everything in their paths. Over and over watching people begging for mercy and for their lives because of all the power we held in our hands. Our time period for attack was small and the blow to them had to be massive.

With time ticking and the feeling in their air of anxious anticipation, I burst into our temporary headquarters to give the order. My hands shook from the exhilaration that was buried within me and that I was trying to contain, as I shot off the flares that would be my order for the start of simultaneous firing from all our weapons. This resulted in the opening of the heaviest bombardment in the whole war so far to date. I said the words that I had been waiting to say for a long time, "it's time now, comrades", I blurted out, trying to gain my composure and not be giddy like a small child.

Within seconds, I heard the sounds of our planes humming. Finally, salvation would be ours! I paced anxiously while the sounds of our planes and bombs boomed loudly, shaking the ground with angry violence. The last forceful movement of the ground caused something behind me to fall over. I quickly turned around to see what it was. Our glorious flag, a symbol of great pride among our people, was lifelessly on the floor. Something that beautiful and magnificent did not belong there. It needed to be put up somewhere high to mark our glorious victory. Someone had to do it. With just the person in mind, I grabbed the flag from the floor and ran as fast as my stocky body would allow me. I scanned for the nearest vehicle and a little ways away, one was sitting there just waiting to get into the action. I jumped in and tried to start the engine, but it just sputtered. Again, I turned the key but nothing. I scanned outside while I tried the key again to see if there was another vehicle I could use, but there was nothing. This was my only hope. "Please start," I begged the engine. I hit the steering wheel with my hands in pure frustration. "Please, God. Let me win this battle with your guidance," I prayed. Then, it indeed happened. With one final turn of the key, the engine quickly purred like a kitten and without a fight. I pressed down on the gas a few times, the engine roaring and ready to go. I put the gear in drive and with all the strength in my right foot, pressed hard on the accelerator. The truck lunged violently forward, dead set on its path and was very responsive to my command. Over many bumps in the rocky terrain we drove through until I saw my men. I slammed on the brake, which caused me to fall forward and roughly back into the seat. My back throbbed from the force, but I ignored it as I grabbed the flag and ran out the door. As I passed my fighting soldiers while I ran to dodge the incoming fire, they looked at me with great concern for my life and with wonder about what I was doing. I just kept right on racing until I saw him. "Vadim, Vadim." He immediately stepped out of line and turned around. I stopped in front of him, desperately trying to catch my breath.

"Sir, what is it?" He curiously questioned me, probably wanting to know why I was running toward him like a madman.

"Take the...flag and put...it on the top...of the...tallest building you...can find," I forced out while gasping for air.

Vadim took the flag very carefully. He smiled at me, seemingly proud and honored that I had asked him to be the representative and carrier of the flag of our great country. "Yes, sir." He saluted and marched off with the flag in his hands, finding his place once again in line. I stood watching my men march ahead, ready to fight whatever was in their path. When they all had filed past me and were long gone, I ran back to the truck. I sat in it for a few moments, staring out in the distance and watching buildings collapse in sync with the rumblings in the ground. I started the engine and proceeded out to the observation post we had built.

I had a second hand account based on what Vadim had told me years later, as to his mission with the flag in Berlin. Vadim said the planes whooshed past, causing Vadim and the other men to cover their ears from the deafening blasts. The power from the explosions were so strong, they all had a hard time keeping themselves upright. Tanks were rolling past them, sending off blasts when they encountered the scrambling Germans. Even though the enemy was running out of steam, they still fought with all their power. There was a ferocious encounter with my army and enemy soldiers. They fired relentlessly at each other, back and forth. There were stray bullets striking the soldiers on both sides, knocking numerous ones down to the ground. Vadim was shooting off his rifle with great force, hungry for German blood. While he was shooting, he looked around at the buildings to find which one would make the most powerful image that the Soviets were victorious, but most of the buildings were in shambles. He forced his way down the streets. German soldiers were popping out from behind walls, cars, and whatever else they could find to shield themselves from enemy view. The flag weighed heavy in his hands and it was difficult to carry it while controlling his gun, but the warrior in him wanted to kill as many of those cowards as possible while carrying out the task I gave him. It felt like a maze, men mixed with machines. Vadim was wildly dodging bullets and being careful not to be trampled by the mammoth tanks, as humans looked like small ants standing next to one of these beasts. He was making his way from out behind a building in a frenzy and realized he stepped right into the path of the Tiger tank. He ran as fast as he could while being shot at from both sides of the street. The tank operators seemed to have spotted him and furiously chased him down. Vadim ran with all the power in his legs. As the giant machine grew closer, its shadow began to swallow him. The machine was now inches from crushing him. He felt like he was taking his last breath, thoughts of his deceased family raced through his mind.

He remembered how he would come home late at night and thought everyone was asleep. He quietly found a little morsel to eat before bed. Before he could sit to eat it, a loud cry rang out from his daughter's room. He bolted out of his chair and into her room so her crying wouldn't wake his wife. His wife's daily chores were difficult enough, so he wanted her to get a restful night's sleep. Also, he rarely saw his daughter with the hours he worked. He wanted to spend quality time with her and be a part of her special moments. He quickly scooped his little bundle of joy up in his arms. "What's wrong, my beautiful little angel?" he asked her. She kept right on wailing. Finally, he decided to take her outside. It was a mild night, not warm and not cold either. He was certain that in their small home, her persistent crying would wake his sleeping beauty.

Once outside, he sat on a wooden rocking chair on their front porch and carefully laid his child down in his arms. She had quieted down a little, but not enough for his liking. He started to gently hum a lullaby his mother used to lull him to sleep with when he was a little child. Even though he couldn't carry a tune, the somewhat melodic song calmed the little one down. As she looked in her papa's eyes and cooed gently at him in contentment, he smiled down at her and stroked her face gently. He looked up at the vast night sky and the little points of light that peeped through the black blanket. "There are so many things I want to show you and teach you Lexi."

"How about you teach her how to say hello to her future spouse when she gets home?" A sweet, angelic voice interrupted him. He turned around to find his wife standing in the doorway. That was one of the things he loved most about her was that humor. She always found the humor, even during the most difficult times. She looked so beautiful standing in the doorway. Her long blonde hair gently flowed around her beautifully angled face. Her big dark eyes always had a sparkle in them that made you feel warm inside. She was such a breathtaking sight, even just awakening from slumber. He truly felt like such a blessed man at that moment, proud in the family unit he had created.

"I'm sorry, darling. I wanted you to sleep," he answered.

"Dear, her wailing was loud enough to wake the entire city. Of course I was going to wake up," she said laughing. He felt badly that his plan hadn't worked out. She must have seen the disappointment on his face and reassuringly chimed, "but I appreciate the thoughtful gesture." She sat down on the ground next to the rocking chair and stroked his arm. "That's why I chose to marry you over the wealthy man who actively pursued me. You have a heart of gold. Although, it might have been nice to have a servant doing this work," she laughed that warm friendly laugh that could make even the most stern person crack a smile.

"I love you," he said passionately to her. She responded by gently kissing his inviting lips.

That was one of the last encounters he had with his family. Back from his memory, a tear rolled from his eye and down his cheek. He had to raise our flag, in honor of his family who was mercilessly killed at the hands of this enemy. Right before the giant tank crushed him, with all the strength he could muster, he flung himself out of the giant's path; his arm hit up against some sharp brick. The pain was excruciating and the sharp edge had cut deeply into skin. The blood dripped down his arm and all around him. As best as he could, he ignored the pain. He had lost the flag in the process of escaping from being crushed by the tank. He wildly searched for the flag in the rubble while the merciless fighting carried on around him. He pushed through rubble and lifted heavy stones. He finally found it, laying a few feet from where he had landed. He picked it up and brushed the dust off and examined the flag. Luckily, there were no tears on the flag. Vadim looked up at the building in front of him. It was a massive pile of brick that had remarkably stayed intact during the blasting. Directly on the top of the pole waved the Nazi flag. Oddly enough, it didn't appear as menacing as it once had with its razor-edged symbol. Now it just looked like a flag with an oddly shaped symbol that stood for a fall from power.

Vadim opened the door and was immediately fired upon. He barely dodged the bullets. Two of his comrades had been watching him and ran over to see what he was doing. "What are you doing?" one of them asked.

"Marshal Zhukov told me to raise our flag on top of the building, but there are Germans inside here. I need help!" The two other men were about to enter through the doorway. "Be careful! They're firing at anyone who enters." The two propped their guns up and slowly peeked in the doorway. Sure enough, bullets rang out once again.

Waiting until the shooting ceased, the two appeared in the doorway and fired. Shots grew louder as the Germans began firing again. One of the men fell to the ground, writhing in pain. He had a bullet hole in his stomach that had blood pouring from it. When Vadim tried to help him he yelled, "Just go!" Vadim and his comrade continued into the building, carefully with their weapons drawn in case they had to ward off additional enemy fire. They climbed the numerous stairs, slowly working their way to the top.

After one flight of stairs, shots again rang out from above them. They both dropped to the floor with a loud thud. Vadim began to grow agitated with this blockade. He left the flag on the ground and while in a ducking position, continued to slink up the stairs. "Take the flag. I'm going up ahead," Vadim called down. He slinked further up the steps. Again, shots rang out. This time though, Vadim fired back with all his strength. This became a pattern, slinking up and shooting. Down like flies the Germans fell and Vadim felt more powerful with each one he killed. His comrade was slowly making his way up behind him, flag in tow. Finally, they reached the door leading out to the roof. Barging it open, the city below them appeared small. They both felt on top of the world. Vadim looked around and found the flagpole. He ran over to it and forced the Nazi flag down with his bare hands. He ripped the flag off the pole. He detached our flag from its existing pole and reattached it to the stationary one on this rooftop. He hurriedly raised it up so it waved proudly in the wind.

The thunderous cheers from down below radiated throughout the city. Seeing our flag waving proudly on top of the building, I dropped my binoculars and hopped into the truck. I stopped right below the building. Everywhere, the Germans had their arms up in a sign of surrender. The city was completely surrounded by our troops.

Just then, Vadim emerged from the building. He had such an animalistic, fiery intensity to him. He slowly walked towards me, but he wasn't looking at me. He was staring directly behind me. I turned around to see what he was looking at. A German officer had his hands up in surrender. He looked to be about forty years old. He had jet black hair and very dark eyes and was scared. He was whimpering something in German, so I obviously couldn't understand what he was saying. The German soldier was visibly frightened as he looked back at Vadim, and Vadim in return was staring the German down like an animal ready to attack. In a flash, Vadim ran at the German and pounced him to the ground. He wildly threw punches at the soldier's face like all the anger and hatred towards the enemy was contained in the strength of his hands. The soldier's face and nose were completely bloodied. It was like with each punch, he gained even more strength until merely punching him was no longer satisfactory. He clasped his hands around the German's neck and squeezed with all his aggression. "You murderer! You killed my family. He squeezed the man's neck harder. "Die, you German. Die! Die!" I couldn't let him kill this man. He would end up in a terrible prison with such isolation that he could only think of his family's death. Yes, it was unfair. He had every right to kill the enemy who robbed him of his family, but murder is murder, especially on an unarmed combatant who is surrendering. I tried pulling him off with all my strength but he was no match for me. "Don't do it, Vadim. It's not going to bring them back," I said, trying to reason with him. The power of my words seemed to break through the darkness that consumed him. He let go of the man's neck. He sobbed loudly as he dropped to the ground in a fetal position. He cried out in obvious emotional pain. I looked up at our flag that waved high above the city and on top of the building. I was so proud of all the men who fought so hard to bring this victory about. I also felt pride in myself for all the victorious battles I had strategized so as to save my country and the world from Hitler's domination. However, we would all not be absolutely safe until Hitler was killed. It was on this day and at that moment in April 1945 I knew just how to do this.

Looking around at all my men who were prematurely celebrating in the street, I cleared my throat. "Our fight isn't over yet!" I shouted. My words echoed off the walls and made my men stop in their tracks. Even Vadim in his distressed state stopped his sobbing and picked himself up off the ground. Now that I had their attention, I continued. "Follow me! We are going to track down Hitler and drag his body through the streets of Moscow!"

Roaring cheers filled the streets of Berlin. I marched forward; fiery determination filled my whole body. My men filed behind me, matching my footsteps with theirs. The sounds of our marching footsteps now bounced off the ruined buildings. In those footsteps, you could hear our desire to carry out our final mission. All I could think about was how badly I personally wanted to wrap my hands around that monster Hitler's neck and ring the life out of him. I wanted to look pure evil straight into the eyes.

In a very short walk, what appeared before us was a monstrous building with towering stone columns and enormous glass windows. It was the Reichstag building that was only one hundred meters from Hitler's bunker. I turned back towards my men and everyone came to a complete halt. I knew this was the building near where the monster was hiding. "Grab your guns and fire through, men!" I ordered.

Immediately, my men let their guns rip through the building. Some of my soldiers, who had kept shells on them, shot at the building, causing loud explosions. Bullets ripped through and the shattered glass rained down on us. One by one, the bullets and shells pounded into the building.

"Stop! Stop!" I yelled. I waved my hands in the air just in case I was not audible over the gunfire. Immediately, there was silence. Dust settled over us, clouding our vision for a few moments. As it cleared, we saw the elaborate building that was now decorated with numerous bullet holes as well as gaping shell holes. The glass that had stood so tall and proud was now shattered and strewn all over the ground in a sea of glistening pieces that were highlighted by the sun.

My men and I poured through the gaping shell holes in the walls and used our bare hands to rip away the debris as we forged forward to reach the area that lay above Hitler's bunker. As we plowed straight through the building to the other side, the daylight exposed the adjacent expanse of land, which looked like a covering for an elaborately large underneath bunker. At the same time, my eye caught the sight of a recessed garden and its obviously heavy, concrete reinforced entrance which masked what I felt was an extensive stairwell to the elaborate bunker below.

In this garden, I now saw the figure of a woman walking through and looking up at the sun whom I recognized as Hitler's mistress, Eva Braun. Then, in one shocking instance, I caught a glimpse of the eyes of a dark haired man with a mustache peering out longingly at Eva as if wanting to join her but was very fearful of doing so. Our eyes met again and I knew I was staring at the face of evil itself in Hitler, and this was no vision. That was it, the moment I had been waiting for. I grabbed my gun and quickly brought it up to aim directly at him, when he slithered, like the dejected snake he was, back into the stairwell.

"Get back in the bunker!" Hitler shouted. Like a whirlwind, Eva raced to the opening of the bunker and the steel door was closed behind her.

"Fire!" I yelled at my men. As if our firing alerted the enemy, German officers immediately began firing upon us in return. These Germans were fighting with their last bout of effort to save their disgraced leader. Fierce firing on both sides persisted. Soldiers on either side of the firing line fell like flies.

After several hours of resistance, we killed the remaining Germans and we broke through with our shells into the steel reinforced door of the concrete bunker that housed the stairwell leading down into the depths of Hitler's bunker. As I entered, a man screamed as he came toward me with his arms up in surrender. "Don't shoot! Don't shoot! I have information for you," pleaded the German voice. "I am Hitler's personal valet, S.S. Major Heinz Ling."

I lowered my gun and looked him straight in the eye. "Speak, quickly!" I ordered him.

The man stood in place, staring at my gun. His eyes looked back up into mine and he continued, "Hitler is dead, Marshal Zhukov. I, personally, witnessed him taking poison and shooting himself in his head along with Eva. She also took poison."

"Bring me to their bodies," I commanded him.

The valet shook his head no. In anger and frustration, I lifted my gun up to his forehead. "You will bring me to the bodies, or I will shoot you."

"Marshal Zhukov, you don't understand. I dragged their bodies out another entrance to an open area and burned the bodies with the extra gasoline that Hitler had ordered and obtained two days earlier." My gun still was held up to his head. He looked at me with great fear. "Please, spare my life."

Nothing would have given me more pleasure then shooting him at that moment, but remembering what I had told Vadim about murder, I lowered my gun. The man let out a giant sigh of relief. I dropped to the ground in exhaustion. "I couldn't even have the satisfaction of dragging Hitler's body through the streets of Moscow. After this long, hard fought war, that's what I wanted to bring to the Soviet people," I said.

"Hitler knew that," the valet said. "Hitler went into a screaming tirade knowing you were coming for him with your army. He said that if he had a General like you, he would have ruled the world. That's why he killed himself."

I looked up at him in shock. I was taken aback by all of this. Even in death, Hitler was a coward. However, it was what he had just said in particular that really stunned me- if he had a general like me, he would have ruled the world. That was my destiny being fulfilled. The evil had been slain and good had triumphed for the world.

NAZI GERMANY IS NO MORE

With Germany left in ruins and Hitler dead, the Nazis soon realized it was fully over for them. No defensive, no resurgence. They were finished. I had been dealing with the temporary head of the fledgling German government they had set up as a means of survival. They tried to negotiate terms where they could keep their dignity and pride, but that was unacceptable. I would only accept full capitulation.

The Nazis finally agreed that Field Marshal Keitel would come and sign the documents on behalf of Germany. That day, I had dressed in my full military uniform with the medals I had earned adorning my chest. I put my cap on and walked into the room. I sat myself at the head of the table. Three soldiers were there with me.

"Should I let him in, Sir?" one of them asked.

I didn't answer him for a few moments. I just sat there contemplating how I would react to seeing him. He was known as the Soviet killer. If he or men under his command encountered a Soviet political or military man, they were shot on the spot. This was all in defiance as to the appropriate and legal acts of war. Taking a deep breath, I tried to relax myself. Repeating this over and over again, I finally got myself in a meditative state that calmed me down. "Send him in," I ordered the soldier.

The soldier opened the door and in walked the pompous man. He was older, probably pushing his sixties. His graying black hair was neatly parted on the side. Marching in proudly, he stopped before me and saluted. I did a once over from his head to his feet. His medals sat there on his chest and it took every ounce of my will power not to rip them off. Medals should be earned for honorable acts and not for acts of massacre. The prolonged silence between the two of us was uncomfortable for him. "Marshal Georgi Zhukov, it is truly an honor to be in your presence. Your military genius is truly commendable."

I simply shot him a dirty look. Flattery wasn't going to spare him. I picked up the surrender documents and set them in front of him. "Read and sign," I said without any emotion, even though I would have loved nothing more than to save the future military tribunal a trial and just shoot him on the spot.

He reached in his pocket and pulled out reading glasses. With great diligence, he sat down in the chair and began perusing through the document page by page. Sometimes he would nod his head in agreement and other times he seemed to sigh in frustration at the face of defeat. When he finished the document, he grabbed the pen that was near him and flowingly signed his name on the unconditional surrender. He closed the document and slid it back in front of me. Taking off his reading glasses, he stood up with a beaming smile on his face. "Well, how about a toast to surrender?"

That statement almost sent me into a tail spin of angered fury. How dare he say that to me! Share a drink with someone who massacred so many people, I would rather be taken out to a field somewhere and be shot from behind. I glared at him to answer his question. Even in his pompous state, he was taken aback by my reaction. "Get out of my sight!" I growled at him.

He saluted me. "Congratulations, sir." The soldier opened the large doors, and the pompous man proudly walked down the aisle and out the doors like he was going to be receiving a big honor. The big honor he ended up receiving was the hangman's noose after he was found guilty for war crimes.

At that moment, I had thought about his congratulations. We had won humanity's survival as we knew it. We were teetering dangerously close to all of our ends. We all had taken a journey through hell and had managed to find our way back to the light. So, yes, congratulations that the light had finally shown on us during humanity's darkest hours was in order.

To celebrate our tremendous triumph, the nations of the United States, Great Britain, and the Soviet Union all met in Frankfurt for a lavish, joyous celebration for the important victory that had been achieved. The soldiers from all three nations had flooded the old German headquarters, a final stab in the heart to the enemy. It was there at the large banquet hall with its elaborate marble floors that we all came together as a united front. The enormous room was damaged from our bombardment of Frankfurt. The once ornate walls were now tattered and torn. The room was truly a mess, but celebrating in the debris was a fitting tribute. All this destruction we had caused put an end to the evil that tried to end us all.

I met someone who became a very close friend of mine until he died- General Eisenhower of the United States. I was speaking to some of our soldiers when I felt a tap on my shoulder. I turned to be greeted by the friendliest eyes I had ever seen. He extended his hand for a shake. "Marshal Zhukov, it's an honor and a privilege to meet you."

"What are you, one of my soldiers to talk to me in such a formal manner? Call me Georgi," I laughed.

I shook his hand and patted him on the back. "The honor is mine, General Eisenhower."

"What are you, one of my soldiers? Call me Ike," he joked back. We shared a good laugh.

All around us, Soviet, American, and British soldiers were warmly greeting each other and sharing tender embraces. It was very heartwarming to see that despite all of our differences in the past, we were able to come together in this joyous time.

There was a giant table set at the front of the room with three large chairs. After exchanging pleasantries with General Montgomery of Britain, I sat in the middle chair with Eisenhower to my left and Montgomery on my right. I never particularly cared for Monty as everyone called him. He was always so stiff and serious. Every time we walked behind him when I was with Ike, I would mock his stiff walk and made a funny face behind his back. Ike would muffle a laugh. Monty would turn around and almost catch me in the act, but my being quick like a jack rabbit; I would straighten up and nod in acknowledgement toward him.

"Hello, old chap," he would say to me, completely oblivious to my mocking him. Then, he would turn around and walk on ahead. Ike and I would just laugh so hard until our stomachs hurt.

After we were all seated, Ike stood up and clinked his glass to get everyone's attention. "I would like to make a toast, first and foremost to a tremendous victory." He raised his glass and I followed suit. Everyone shouted with joy. Then, being the charismatic leader he was, he simply put his finger up to his lips and everybody quieted down within a few seconds. "Now, I want to propose a toast to my good friend Marshal Georgi Zhukov. To no one man do the united nations owe a greater debt than to him for the defeat of Nazi fascism."

Once again, loud roars rang out with the loudest ones being from my soldiers. Three men came into the room, each one holding a flag from their country. They put their flags in a holder next to each other, and there our flags stood. It was funny how the flags were arranged in the same order that the three of us were sitting in at the head table. The applause was so deafening. Happy whistling rang through my ears.

Now, Ike clinked his glass to quiet everyone. Once again, everyone quieted down immediately. "To show the appreciation on behalf of the President of the United States of America, I present to you these two medals of honor." I stood up and he pinned them both on my chest. We shook hands and a photographer came up to take our picture. When he was finished, we sat down and watched our men who were now dancing to Soviet music. I sipped my wine and had a shot of vodka. However, that was nothing compared to Monty, who was downing drinks like they were water.

I laughed and turned my attention back to Ike. "The Normandy invasion you organized was brilliant. I was very impressed with the operation," I said to him.

"I appreciate that, especially coming from you," Ike answered. "But in all my years in military involvement, that was the hardest thing I ever had to plan and organize. What made it so difficult was the timing. Timing was everything. We came dangerously close in failing to time it just right, but I guess the good Lord was on our side."

"We all came dangerously close to failing," I said. "But with all the destruction that was done, how do you ever really get over that?"

"You never really do," Ike said.

"I don't think our country will ever really know just how many lives were lost. From all the damage and the different execution methods that were carried out, I just can't imagine how many people perished," I responded to him.

I watched the men dancing gleefully, kicking their legs up and locking their arms while dancing in circles around each other. I started clapping my hands to the music and nodding my head. I smiled at two soldiers who waved in merriment at me. Then, my attention turned to the American and Soviet flags that stood side by side. Our two countries were now the most powerful countries to emerge from the rubble. "You know," I said to Ike, "our two nations need to remain allies so none of this will ever happen again."

Ike smiled and raised his glass. "A toast to friendship."

I raised my glass and clinked his. "To friendship." I drank another shot of vodka. The room started to spin a little and I felt very dazed. However, I wasn't going to let my drunkenness spoil my fun. I stood up and headed for the dance floor.

"Where are you going"? Ike asked me.

"To show these men how to really dance," I responded.

I went out to the middle of the floor, and my presence caused everyone to stop. They looked confused at me, trying to figure out what I was doing. The music stopped playing and it was so silent, you could hear a pin drop. I looked around and laughed. "Don't worry. I won't bark your head off. Now, play the music." The music immediately started up again. I bowed to my audience and started to move across the floor with gentle strides and then I kicked up my legs. "Hey! Hey!" I yelled while kicking up my legs. This lightened the mood and all the men slowly came back onto the dance floor. We all were heartily dancing and I locked my arms with a different soldier as I tossed myself around the dance floor. We laughed and danced the night away until the early morning hours. All the problems we had faced over the last few years truly seemed to be far in the past and completely out of our minds as we kicked up our legs with each dance move.

THE BEGINNING OF THE END FOR ME

Reflecting back on everything that has happened to me, I could truly say that the next sign of trouble with Stalin was at our Victory Parade in Moscow in late, June of 1945. I had returned for just that week to partake in the festivities before I had to return to Berlin to represent the Soviet Union. It was a joyous occasion, even though the weather was overcast. The air was warm and a gentle breeze flowed past my face. All along the streets, civilians were lined up to celebrate this most joyous occasion. The elderly were mixed in with the very young. That seemed to be representative of our country's journey, from the elderly who had seen what had happened in the past and how we got to this point, to the young who were the future of our country and one of the main reasons why we fought in this war. The sea of anxious and excited people was a very pleasant sight compared to the pain and suffering that I had seen on so many of these faces before.

A group of men with musical instruments marched out first and stopped below the viewing beam. This beam was where Stalin and other high ranking officials stood to deliver speeches and look down at the masses. I think this high beam helped feed into Stalin's ego and power hungry ways. The musicians picked up their instruments and our national anthem came melodiously pouring out.

A car rolled slowly down the road and there inside was the menacing Stalin. Everyone still cheered, although it sounded forced for fear of him. He got out of his car, trailing behind two guards. They slowly marched behind the giant wall and a few minutes later appeared at the top of the beam. Stalin stopped directly in front of the podium and began waving. People were cheering so loudly that you could probably hear them from many miles away. Stalin lifted his arm up straight in the air with his fist clenched, and I knew what that was the signal for.

A sea of soldiers began to pour into the square like the sea coming in for high tide. It was nice to see this wave of proud soldiers rather than Hitler's water flood that would be used to drown us all. The soldiers were lined up perfectly in rows and they marched in perfect rhythm with their rifles. All you could hear were the shoes of the soldiers clapping on the pavement. All the spectators were in awe. In a perfectly uniform fashion, the front row of soldiers stopped, and each subsequent row behind stopped directly behind the other until all of them were perfectly still standing on the pavement.

This was my cue. My horse's handler came out with the trusty steed. The horse was a magnificent creature. His coat was pure white, the color of the snow that has freshly fallen on the ground on a cold winter day. His long, flowing mane that matched the color of his coat was swaying in the breeze. His big, brown almond eyes were scared and wild at the same time. I think the animal sensed my anxiety when he was in my presence, and he started rearing up on his powerful hind legs and kicking his front legs out wildly, almost knocking his handler onto the ground. I motioned for his handler to let me have him. I grabbed his reins and he powered himself into the air once again. This time when he came down, I gently stroked his coat and shushed him. His nostrils were flaring wildly. This horse was the perfect fit for a warrior to ride, his wild spirit just needed to be tamed. When I felt he was in a calmer manner, I put my foot into the stirrup and heaved myself over the massive animal. As soon as my bottom hit his back, he reared up once again. This was a strong animal. Through my legs, I could feel his bulging muscles. I was very high up in the air, but I refused to look down to see just how far up we were. If I had done that, the horse would feel more in power. I simply remained still and calm on his back. A horse and a human have an amazing unspoken communication between the two, and how you achieve that is through body language. I needed him to feel he could trust me.

When he came back to the ground and was more at ease, I gave him a swift kick in the side and he took off cantering. With the wind whipping in my face, I was almost blinded so as not to see any of the soldiers or spectators. I knew they were all watching me with adoring and proud eyes. I sat up even straighter in my saddle and continued cantering past the soldiers. Now, loud cheers rang out as I rode up to the beam and stopped my horse. I got off in one motion and walked up to it. Behind the wall were numerous stairs leading up to the platform of the beam. They were very tiny steps, barely big enough to fit one's toe. I climbed each of these little nuisances until I reached the top. There Stalin stood waiting for me and watching me very carefully. He extended his hand to shake mine, but it wasn't a warm, friendly greeting. It was more of a formality and a ceremonial gesture than anything else. I walked up to the speaking podium to deliver my speech. Looking down at everyone, I could see that everyone was paying particular attention to me. With that, I delivered my speech. "Working men and women, farm workers, workers in science, technology, and the arts, fellow soldiers...I greet you on the occasion of our great victory over German Imperialism. Thanks to the united efforts of the great powers, our great nation, the United States of America, and Great Britain, Fascist Germany has been reduced to dust!"

It was a short and simple speech, but I think it made my point. The roaring cheers and thunderous applause corroborated this for me. Everyone started chanting. At first, it sounded like a cacophony of noise. Soon my ears adjusted and I could hear what they were saying. "Zhukov, Zhukov, Zhukov." I waved to the crowd and the thunderous cheers grew louder.

As I waved, I felt like someone was staring at me intently. The soldiers were shooting guns into the air. With each shot, the staring felt like daggers in my back. While the celebration continued below me, I slowly turned around to see who it was that was looking at me. Stalin was standing there glaring at me with jealousy. This look stayed ingrained in my mind. The look was very cold and evil and with every chant of my name became more intense. We had a stare down until he interrupted it by calling over the sniveling Beria. Stalin whispered something in his ear and they both looked up at me while talking. They were discussing something about me and I didn't have a good feeling about it. It was the feeling in the pit of my stomach that was trying to warn me and tell me something was wrong, but the chants broke through my concentration and reminded me of the tremendous happiness and relief we all were feeling. I turned back around and waved to the crowd, so as to take in all this glory that I knew I deserved. Little did I know this would be my last hoorah and momentous occasion.

Soon after that parade, I was assigned to head and control the Soviet sector of Berlin. The United Nations were trying to deal with the aftermath and clean up of Germany. The German people were like a ship without a rudder. They needed direction, but a major power struggle was happening. Stalin had a major distrust among the other members of our council. He felt President Truman and Churchill were collaborating in an effort to push us further out of the loop and capture more influence in the region to satisfy their own selfish power.

I was thinking about this one day as I worked in my office. I was organizing the minutes I had written at the council meeting. Putting them in carefully one at a time, there was a knock at my door.

"General Eisenhower is here to see you, Sir," my secretary said.

"Send him in," I said. She exited the room and a few moments later my dear friend walked in, but he had a very troubled look on his face instead of his usual friendly demeanor. "What's the matter?" I questioned.

He looked at me blankly then walked over to the window. My office had a beautiful view of Berlin and the skyline, but the view also showed the ruins the city lay in. It almost served as a reminder of how important our task was there. This was the way Germany was left after the First World War. With the demoralization of the German population, it was easy for Hitler to manipulate their minds and emotions and rise to power. We couldn't let another madman take control ever again. That's why it was so vital for us to work efficiently to fix the problems in carving a path to a better future for the Germans.

"Stalin is being increasingly difficult and we can't get anything done," Eisenhower finally said.

I got up from my chair and went out the door. I went up to my secretary's desk. "Hold all my calls," I said to her. I had a feeling I was going to have a heart to heart with Ike, so I used the excuse to talk to my secretary to examine my surroundings. I wanted to check to make sure no one was eavesdropping or could eavesdrop. On that particular day, there weren't a lot of people in the building. A few lower level officials were walking past me, carrying folders. They appeared harmless, so I went back into my office and shut the door, swiftly locking it. I went back to my desk and sat down. Ike had been curiously watching me. He decided to follow suit and sat down in one of the chairs at my desk. He took off his hat, revealing his balding head. He put the hat on my desk and sank back in the chair, crossing his right leg over his left. He sighed and looked up at me. "So what is it you want me to do?" I asked him.

"Talk to Stalin, put some sense into him or something. He's making all these wild accusations and it's ridiculous. We've withdrawn our troops from where he requested, to put him at ease, and he's still not happy.

I wanted so badly to tell him that of course Stalin is unyielding! He kills people for no reason and not just anybody, but he purged high ranking Commanders of our army based on phantom nonsense. He thinks everyone is out to get him. If you cough the wrong way, he would probably think it's a signal for someone to jump out from behind the wall to put a bullet into his brain, only the one who coughed would end up with the bullet in his head instead. Stalin belongs in an institution and someone should throw away the key. No, I wouldn't dare say that aloud to Ike, for I would be the one killed for saying anything ill willed against the Premier. "I'll try to see what I can do," I ended up responding to him.

"Somehow, I don't think that's going to be enough," Ike said.

His statement took me aback. It wasn't so much what he said, but how he said it. I knew he had something much more serious in mind. "What makes you think that?"

He got up from the chair and walked back over to the window. He put his arms behind his back and stood perfectly straight for a few moments. "I may be speaking out of place here, and forgive me if I do, but I feel it's necessary to speak my mind."

"Of course, go ahead," I said.

He took in a deep breath and exhaled very slowly. "I, well, we all feel that you should take over as Premiere."

I just sank back in my chair like a useless entity. I was so stunned by this assertion that I didn't even know how to respond. I just stared at his back for what felt like a long time. "No," I simply muttered.

"Something can be arranged if..."

"Stop it!" I jumped out of my chair and ran over to him. "Are you trying to get me killed?"

Ike just kept staring out the window as he muttered, "No."

Feeling guilty about snapping at my friend, I calmed my voice. "I appreciate that you and everyone else seem to think so highly of me, but I'm a military man. There's no place for me in politics. Politics and military issues don't mix. That's what the problem comes from. You understand what the right thing to do is, but those political issues stop it from happening. If the politicians would stay out of it and let us military men do our work, everything would be fine."

Ike turned to look at me. "But if this continues, there's going to be trouble."

"Yes, I know. But there's nothing I can do. I have to do what Stalin wants. I can't get involved in these political situations. Believe me, if it had anything to do with a military enemy,

I would be the first one in his office, and I would force him to listen. But what you're talking about now, is none of my business."

When Ike turned to look at me, the portrait above the door caught his attention. My eyes followed his. Stalin stared down at us with cold, dark eyes. The artist had ignored the horrible scars on his face and given him skin as smooth as a porcelain doll. I turned my attention away from the portrait and back to my old friend. "Would you like some tea? I'm brewing some.

"Yes." Ike returned to his seat across from me. "Thank you."

I went out to our kitchen area to retrieve the tea. Gently, I took out two cups and poured the boiling water into each one. I decorated the side of the cups with the tea bags. Walking back into the room, Ike was looking at a photo of my wife and oldest daughter. I placed the tea on the desk in front of him. "You have a beautiful family," he said to me.

I looked at the photo. My wife was sitting down with little Alexa on her lap. Alexa was wearing a beautiful white laced dress and had a ribbon decorating her hair. Her eyes were so bright and youthful and she looked blissfully happy and yet very curiously at the camera. "I do have a lovely family that I miss very much. Do you have any children?"

"I have a son John. He's serving in the army. I'm very proud of him. But I had...a son Doud. He died when he was three from scarlet fever." He looked down, trying to stop himself from shedding a tear."

"Oh God, I'm so sorry." I was very flattered he felt close enough with me to share an intimate detail of his life with a fellow General.

Ike immediately perked up and smiled. "Hey, when this is all over, we should go fishing together. Do you like to fish?"

"One of my favorite things to do," I answered

"Great! I should head back to headquarters. They're probably lost without me over there," he laughed. I walked him to my door and exchanged a friendly handshake with him. He began to walk off, but stopped in front of my secretary's desk. He turned back around. "By the way, I have a gift for you." He smiled at me and continued walking.

That appeared to be a cue for my secretary.

She jumped out of her chair with a box in her hands. "General Eisenhower wanted me to give this to you," she said.

I took the box out of her hands. "Thank you," I said. Then, I went back into my office and sat down at my desk to open the box. It was carefully sealed and hard to open. I went into my desk and retrieved a letter opener to carefully slice through the seal. Once the box was open, I noticed a letter inside. I picked it up to read it. "Georgi, I extend this journal to you as a token of my appreciation to not only a brilliant General, but a dear friend. I hope you use it to write all your brilliant stories in it and anything else you would like to share and it's my sincerest hope that the world will be lucky to one day read it, with great respect, Ike".

I smiled and put down the letter to retrieve the contents of the box. I pulled out a beautiful red journal with the gold letters embroidered "The Truthful Memoir by Marshal Georgi Zhukov. I opened it up to find numerous blank, snow white pages. I leafed through the pages, enjoying the newness of this journal.

Immediately, I pulled a piece of paper from my desk to write him a letter of gratitude for the generous gift, but an uneasy feeling consumed me. I looked back up at the Stalin portrait. His eyes felt even colder as they watched me. I could sense that trouble was brewing, but what kind of trouble it was I wasn't exactly sure at that time.

I would later find out from my confidante who told me what happened back in Moscow at this same time. This is how the events occurred as they were told to me.

Stalin was at his desk. While at his desk, the sniveling weasel of a man Beria came into his office carrying numerous newspapers in his arms. Beria, with my confidante in the room said, "Premier Stalin, have you seen these?"

"Why are you interrupting me with newspaper nonsense?" Stalin angrily snapped at Beria and lunged out of his chair, grabbing the papers from his arms. A few fell on the floor. "Pick them up!" He ordered. Beria, like the obedient and pathetic lapdog he was, got down on his hands and knees and followed Stalin's orders. Meanwhile, Stalin carefully read the papers. His eyes appeared to narrow in anger at what he saw. "Marshal Zhukov, the Marshal of Victory. Where you find Zhukov, you find victory. Zhukov, the most popular figure of our great country," he read them all aloud. When Stalin read the last sentence, his anger appeared to boil over. "Marshal Zhukov, a possible successor to Stalin." With all his force and rage, he threw the papers across the room. They all floated around in the air until they slowly zigzagged down and littered the floor.

Beria, who was still on the floor, started picking up the papers like he was a mind reader and knew this was what Stalin wanted him to do.

"Sir, Zhukov is dangerous. Look at all the support he has from the people. Don't you think he could overthrow you with ease?". Beria stopped cleaning for a minute. "I've also heard there are letters," Beria said in a lowered voice.

Still with that infamous evil look on his face, but now mixed with curiosity and anxiety, Stalin asks "what letters?"

"The letters discussing how he is going to carry out his plans, mostly with the American Eisenhower. He's even received gifts from other countries to encourage him to do it." Stalin's face became a deeper shade of red with each wave of rage that appeared to overcome him. "What can I do to him, something that will rightfully punish him?"

"Why don't you let me kill him? How about I shoot one bullet right in the back of his head? He'll never even know what happened to him." Beria stood up from the floor with great excitement like his master was giving him a dog treat. "Or I could shoot one right in his heart while he's looking. Then, you can watch the lousy traitor die right in front of your own eyes."

"We can't kill him! He's far too popular with the people, and as much as I hate to admit it, he has done an outstanding job winning the war."

Beria was upset that his master, Stalin, wasn't giving him enough attention and praise for wanting to be rid of me, Marshal Zhukov. After all the praise from the newspapers, I was a pest to Beria. I was a reminder to Beria that he was nothing and did not a thing but be obedient. Beria hated me because he alone wanted to be gold in Stalin's eyes. Beria continued to say, "Then why don't we have a trial, and once Zhukov is convicted, we take him out and have him shot by the firing squad."

Stalin's eyes lit up at this suggestion like a light bulb had gone off in his head. Stalin said to Beria, "I want you to gather all the evidence you have against him and get an eyewitness to say he saw with his own eyes and heard with his own ears that all of this happened as you say."

"I'll gather everything you need, Sir." Beria marched out of Stalin's office to get to work. He went into his office and sat at his desk. "I'll give him evidence," he said in a conniving and devious way. He picked up a blank piece of paper on the desk and began to write. Scratching noises from the pen meandering its way on the paper was the only noise that could be heard in the room other than his own delayed breathing, because he was careful about how he was writing. While he wrote, he was looking at another paper right next to it. He carefully glanced back and forth while he made his gentle strokes. When he finished with that one, he picked up another blank paper and began to copy once again. He continued doing this until he had a dozen papers finished.

Putting the papers in a neat stack, he gently placed his pen down right next to it and got up out of his chair. He walked down the hall where a couple of guards were on break. They were smoking cigarettes and playing cards. "Get up! We have someone to pay a visit to who will give us evidence against Zhukov," Beria barked at them. Beria seemed to feel good ordering someone else around instead of being ordered around himself.

Beria and the guards went to visit a good friend and comrade who I had worked closely with throughout the war. I don't want to mention his name to respect his wishes to remain anonymous. This is the story he related to me as to what took place next.

That same night, my good friend was at home reading a book in his study. He was interrupted by a knock at the door. "Come in," he said.

His wife slowly opened the door, carrying a glass of water. "I thought you'd want something to drink, honey."

He put down his book and took off his reading glasses. He stood up to take the glass from her. Gently putting the glass down on his table, he walked up behind his wife and started caressing her arms. "You're so thoughtful," he said gently into her ear.

"Well, I thought I would show just how much I love you."

He gave her gentle kisses on her cheek. "I can think of another way you can show how much you love me."

She turned to face him and their two welcoming lips met in a warm, wet embrace. They were deeply involved in this tender moment when a burst of high energy interrupted them. The pitter patter of small feet ran right past them.

"Papa! Papa!" the little boy was yelling and dancing around.

My comrade and his wife parted their lips and he sighed in frustration that they couldn't continue their intimacy. "Come here you little monster," he said in a playful way to his little son.

"Stop reading and come spend time with mommy and me," he said in a demanding voice, but it was too cute and squeaky to take seriously. My comrade looked up at his wife and then back to his son. "Did mommy put you up to that?"

The little boy hesitated for a minute and then said innocently "maybe."

"Maybe, huh, maybe I should tickle you." He gently massaged his fingers into the little boy's stomach causing an eruption of giggles.

"No. No," the little boy pleaded through his giggles.

My comrade stopped and sat his son on his lap. He gently kissed his head and gave him a hug. "Do you want me to read you a bedtime story tonight?"

"Yeah!" the boy shouted out excitedly.

They were suddenly interrupted by a loud banging on the door. My comrade and his wife looked startled at each other. "Who could that be at this hour?" His wife questioned. She walked to the front door to answer it. "Who's there?" She called out to the mystery person who knocked.

"It's the police. Open up this door at once!" Beria answered.

Even though she was frightened and confused by this unexpected response, she obeyed by unlatching the lock and twisting the knob. "What is this about?"

Beria stormed right past her with the two police guards behind him. "Where is your husband?"

"He's in his office, but I demand to know what this is about!"

Beria ignored her, dead set on his mission to retrieve his victim for his evil plan and to get into Stalin's good graces.

My comrade took his son off his lap and sat him on the couch. He was frightened why Beria and two officers were there. Wherever Beria was, trouble was always right there. "What are you doing here?" He sees his wife standing in the doorway watching. She looked fearful and tears were welling up in her eyes. The two officers begin ransacking his office, tearing everything in their path apart. His son was so upset from the noise; he covered his ears to block it all out. "How dare you come in here like this and upset my family! If you need to deal with me, then you deal with me privately outside," he yelled at the men. He was a man desperately trying to protect his family, but knew that there was trouble ahead.

Beria whistled at the officers and they stopped what they were doing. He pointed to the little boy. One of the officers grabbed the child by his hair. The child was screaming in fear. My comrade's wife was crying, not knowing how to help her child. The officer wrapped his arm around the boy's neck and took out his gun, putting it up to the boy's head. Beria walked up behind my comrade. "You're under arrest! You are going to come with me willingly and pleasantly otherwise you will be responsible for your little brat's brains being all over your couch."

"Please, leave my son alone! Your issue is with me and not him," my comrade pleaded with them. He was wildly coming up with a plan to kill these men. Beria was a smaller man and appeared to be without a gun, but the two guards were big men and armed. My comrade's gun was right underneath the couch. If he dropped to the floor quickly, he would be shot at or even worse, his son would be shot.

"Go search for the papers," Beria said to the other officer. He immediately continued the ransacking. With Beria watching this and the officer holding his son so both were distracted, my comrade slowly went to the floor to reach under the sofa for his gun. When he reached under, the floor made a loud creaking noise. Beria turned to see what was happening. "What are you doing?" He shouted.

"I thought I dropped something," he answered.

Beria glared at him. He looked down at the couch and briskly walked over to it. Dropping to the floor, he reached underneath and moved his hand around until he felt the weapon. He pulled it out from the couch and stood up to look at it. "Is this what you wanted to get?" My comrade just stared at the gun silently, not sure how to answer. With great force, Beria smacked the gun across his face. He dropped to the floor, stunned and in great pain. Blood trickled down from his cheek. "Kill the child. Maybe that will teach him a lesson," Beria said to the guard.

His wife started screaming. He crawled on his hands and knees over to Beria's feet. "No! Don't do it! I made a mistake! I'm sorry! I'll do anything you want, but please don't hurt him!"

Beria motioned for the ransacking guard to come over to where he was standing. He obeyed and picked my comrade up off the floor. He dragged him up to where his son was. His son was crying and fearful. Beria came up to them. "Now you're going to watch your son die," he said.

The guard unlocked the gun and pulled the trigger. The bullet blasted through the boy's head. Blood had splattered on the wall.

His wife screamed out and came running into the room. She tried to attack the guard who shot her son, but he shoved her down on the floor like it was nothing.

Beria walked out the door and the guards obediently followed, dragging my comrade along. They went outside to a car that was waiting. One of the guards opened the car door and threw my comrade inside. Then, Beria and the two piled in.

"Put the blindfold on him," Beria ordered. The guard sitting next to my comrade grabbed something behind the seat. He twisted him around and from behind put a piece of cloth over his eyes. Feeling every bump in the road, my comrade sat there in total darkness. The only thing he saw was the image of his son being murdered in front of his eyes. Repeatedly, it played in his brain and he could see it in his eyes.

After a long ride, the car came to a screeching halt. He could hear the doors opening and a firm hand grabbed his arm and dragged him out of the car. He fell to the ground, and was picked up and dragged again. Going down stairs he almost tripped and fell, but was held up by the guard. Finally, they stopped dead in their tracks.

A door creaked and he was led in. "Sit down," a serious booming voice ordered him. He bent his knees and started to squat down, when a shrieking noise came from the floor. His squatting position was intercepted by the chair that hit his bottom. Someone was moving the blindfold behind his head and then took it off. The air blasted his now bare eyes that were free from the warmth of the cloth, and the cool air now caused him to wince. Even though the bare room was scarcely lit, his eyes still fought hard to adjust. Beria was standing in front of him, staring him down. My comrade was stricken with grief and emotionally drained. "What do you want from me?" he asked.

"You know Marshal Zhukov was plotting to overthrow Premier Stalin. I need you to testify to that."

"What? He never planned anything! Zhukov is loyal to both Premier Stalin and the Party."

Beria walked behind him. My comrade just stared straight ahead like a zombie until he felt a blunt force hit him in the back of the head and knocked him out of the chair. The room was spinning and a sharp pain shot through his head. He cried out in agony. "You will say Zhukov is planning to overthrow Stalin.".

"I swear to you that he's not. I won't say something so untrue about someone I admire and respect."

Beria's impatience seemed to take over. He kicked my comrade in the stomach with hard and swift ones that dug deep into his insides and pierced his stomach.

He violently coughed and blood came up. "Just...kill me. I have...nothing to live...for."

In a fit of rage, Beria picked him up and punched him in the face with sharp jabs of his knuckles. His face was covered in bruises and cuts, and his eyes were swollen. "If you don't admit to it, I'll kill off your little wife," Beria whispered in his ear.

My comrade cried in tears of pain and helplessness. "Yes, it's true. Zhukov's only...goal...in joining...the military was...to be Premier."

Beria dropped him to the ground. He was gasping desperately for air. Beria watched him suffering, appearing to receive evil viewing pleasure. "Good. Now, when we put Zhukov on trial, you're going to tell this directly to Stalin. Do you understand me?"

"You can...tell him...yourself," my comrade coughed out the words."

Angered by this statement, Beria ripped off his belt and put it around my comrade's neck. He pulled it tightly, and the gagging of my comrade caused him to tighten it more. "You WILL appear in front of Stalin and tell him EXACTLY what you told me or I'm going to repeat what I'm doing now on your wife, and I'm going to enjoy watching the life get sucked out of her. But I'm going to finish the job." He released the belt from his neck and pushed him back on the floor.

"I'll do...whatever...you want just...don't hurt...my wife," he said desperately wheezing and gasping for air.

Beria laughed at this pathetic sight of this man bordering death and begging for mercy. He walked over to one of the officers who were standing in the corner, watching this torture happening in front of him. "Give me enough time and I can make someone admit they're the King of England.". They both shared a laugh. "Take him to a cell." He smirked, appearing to be pleased by what he had just done.

While all this was going on, I had been in Berlin for almost a full year when I was suddenly called to return to Moscow. I thought I was being called back because my assignment had been completed and there was nothing else I could do in Berlin. In the back of my mind, I feared it might be that Stalin had discovered my secret which I had been keeping all of these years.

That dreadful day I remember so clearly that it haunts me every night when I'm asleep. I was at my home in Moscow, sitting in the rose garden. The roses were in full bloom, and they were the color of a woman's lips after she had newly applied her lipstick. The leaves were a deep shade of fresh green. The colors were aesthetic and to complement this, I decided to play my accordion. Playing it was always a type of therapy for me. It helped me escape from any stress and worry and just allowed me to relax. I began playing it and the melodious noise filled my ears. Birds chirped along with the music, perhaps thinking it was another creature pleading with them to call out their beautiful, natural songs. All this nature and music was so enjoyable, I started humming. With each pull and push of the accordion, I swayed my shoulders to accompany my humming. The birds were flying around while they sang, calling out to other birds to join in as the chorus. Now, the relaxation I had set out to accomplish, I in fact did. Lost in the ballad, my mind escaped into a blank world. I literally had no thoughts except for the notes of the song playing in my head.

All that was interrupted when I felt a tap on my shoulder. Like a domino effect, I stopped playing the accordion and everything else stopped one by one after that. Startled, I turned around to see one of Stalin's officers curiously looking at me. I guess he didn't find my song and dance particularly entertaining. "Marshal Zhukov, Premier Stalin requests to see you immediately.

"What is this concerning?" He didn't answer me. He just looked at me stone faced. I was a little irritated that I was ignored. "I need to know what's going on," I pressed him to try and gather some inkling as to what purpose I was being called on for.

"Just come with me," he said, digging his heels into my persistence.

"Fine, but let me put my accordion inside. I want to leave a message with my family to let them know I have left for a little while."

"I'm sorry, Marshal Zhukov, but Premier Stalin wants to see you at once and will not wait for you to do mundane tasks."

"I'm going to do these things and you will wait for me!" I refused to be bossed around by someone of a lower rank than I was."

He merely nodded his head in agreement. I went inside my home and placed my accordion down on the chair next to my desk where I always kept it. I ripped off a piece of paper and quickly jotted down that I was out and not to worry about me. Then I pondered for a moment. Should I be worried? What if there was something wrong? That uneasy feeling came back to me until I caught my medals in the corner of my eye. Look at all those medals. The way they shone and how much they portrayed me as the hero I was. Stalin was probably going to give me more medals for honor and bravery. I decided to put on my full military uniform to make a proper showing and be able to place these medals on my already highly decorated chest. I walked out to the officer. "I'm ready," I said happily and proudly.

We walked off to a black car. I nodded at the chauffeur who opened the door for me. I sat in the backseat, anxiously waiting to leave. The chauffeur shut the door and stood outside talking to the officer in a deep conversation. It did strike me as odd that they were speaking in this manner, but I didn't give it much thought at the time. After a few moments, they got in the car and we drove off.

During the whole car ride, I thought about if I should prepare a quick mental speech in my mind. I could say I was truly humbled by this honor. Thank you to my fellow soldiers for whose tireless effort and courageous hearts will always be remembered and appreciated. However, then, I would have to praise Stalin. The only praise he deserved was doing a good job of murdering innocent people and almost causing us to be ruled by the German Nazis. I was thinking of Stalin right at the time we were approaching his office, which is where he usually gave out the country's medals. As I watched, we drove past his office and I became puzzled. "Where are we going? I thought we were going to the Premier's office?" I questioned the officer who was sitting in the front seat next to the chauffeur.

"You're going somewhere else," he answered without any emotion.

"Where?" I demanded.

The officer turned around to face me. He was clearly aggravated with my interrogation of him. "You'll find out soon enough."

The car came to a stop and I looked out. We arrived at the building that appeared as a military library on the surface, but boiling underneath was a secret meeting chamber where highly classified dealings took place. I was more concerned than ever because this is where the "trials" were held for the massacred Commanders before the war, if you could even call them trials. They were more like an intentional, negative campaign against the accused, who was not able to protect himself from the filth being thrown at him. My car door was opened and I slowly slinked my way out like some poor, defenseless animal that was beaten by its master only to now have to face its abuser once again.

The officer led me up the long steps to the front doors. He opened them and we walked past the numerous books on the shelves, and yet, the place felt completely barren without any people there. As we walked down the long hallway, I couldn't help feel like I was being led to my execution. It was as if I had gone back in time and replaced my old dearly departed comrade on his death walk. I could feel how scared and lost he was as he took those same steps as I took now. The officer looked around then pulled out the big book on the shelf. It started shaking violently, almost causing the books to be knocked off. The bookshelf slid open very gently to reveal a passageway once it stopped its rumblings. He walked down the dimly lit hallway and what other choice did I have but to follow. Our steps echoed through the hollow halls.

As we came up to the silver doors, my heart raced from the anticipation of what was on the other side of the door. He could have just opened the door and a gun would go off, the bullet piercing my heart and me falling to the ground cold. When he opened the door, it was much more intimidating. I was led into the room with heads of the Party, other non-authoritative members of the Party, and some high ranking army officials who were placed in seats with the lower rows at ground levels and the other rows a little higher up behind them. The top rows were very close to the ceiling of the room. Stalin sat at the very front in his seat of honor and the sniveling, little Beria sat just below him on his left. All these men were looking down upon me. The officer led me down the long floor in a straight line with Stalin's chair. All these men were watching me with steadfast eyes. I felt like an ant on a hill with a bunch of humans watching as I, this little ant, carried out my chores for the ant hill. We stopped in front of Stalin's chair but I was still standing in the middle of the bare floor so everyone could keep looking down upon me. The officer walked away and really left me all alone. I looked around at everyone who was looking down at me now with disapproving looks.

Stalin cleared his throat and I turned around to stare at the familiarly menacing figure. "Marshal Zhukov, you are brought here today to stand trial for very serious accusations against you."

I think I stopped breathing for a moment because, when I tried to speak, I had to cough and breathe in to catch my breath. "What sort of accusations?" I asked. I glanced over all the men around me. Which one of these men would ever say anything bad against me? Then my attention turned to Beria, the lap dog sitting on the left of Stalin.

"Accusations of treason. Very serious treason," Stalin said.

I was stunned and horrified at the same time. I took all this emotion out on that dog, Beria, as I glared at him. He didn't wince back with his tail tucked between his legs. He merely sat there proudly with his head held high. "What sort of treason am I falsely being accused of?" I asked not taking my eyes off of Beria.

"Conspiracy to overthrow me and MY position of power," Stalin growled at me.

"What? That's a lie! I would never do such a thing. Look at all I've done for you, for the Party. Why would I do that if I wanted to overthrow you?"

"Then why are you receiving gifts from the American Eisenhower and from Britain. They're sending these to you to encourage my ouster!" Stalin wildly shot back.

"No! General Eisenhower is a very good friend of mine and he gave me a gift as a token of his friendship. I received gifts from Britain as a token of their appreciation for my efforts in the war. That's it. For no other reason, I assure you!"

Stalin leaned out of his chair further. "Then why do I have an eyewitness with valid, tangible proof?" he said in a lowered more accusatory tone.

"What? Who would ever say that? There's nothing to show because I've never done what you say I did!"

Stalin just ignored me and turned his attention to the back of the room. "Send him in," he shouted. The doors creaked opened and I looked to see what everyone's eyes were now looking at. There, being dragged in by my officer was my comrade who I had previously spoken about. His head was down and further away so I wasn't able to see his face fully until he came closer to me and I could tell you I was horrified by his appearance. His face was covered in cuts and black and blue marks. His eyes were swollen and I could tell they were met by fists.

"What did you do to him?!" I screamed at Beria.

"His home was robbed and he fought off the intruder but unfortunately his son was killed in the process," Stalin answered instead.

All I could think of was how sorry I was for him. When my comrade heard this about his son, his head dropped down. He was standing a good forty feet from me and I couldn't tear my eyes off of him. His internal pain and suffering was so transparent to me through his clothes, skin, everything.

"Premier Stalin, members of the Party," Beria started and stood up. I turned my attention to him and glared once again. "I have in my hand a correspondence written by Marshal Zhukov discussing his options of how he was going to overthrow the Premier. Gentlemen of the Party, if this is not proof that indeed Marshal Zhukov was involved, then I don't know what else will do. Our witness here will corroborate this as he told me."

My attention turned back to my comrade, and like he was following a script he began immediately after Beria finished. "It's true that Marshal Zhukov wrote that letter. I saw him do it. He's always said he could lead our country better than Premier Stalin and this was his only chance to do so."

My eyes grew wide at the horrible lies that were coming from his mouth. "I want to see that letter," I demanded. Beria came down from his high perch and walked over to me. He handed the letter to me, confident that his fallacious libel and slander against me had worked. I shot him a look and snatched the paper from his hand. Carefully gliding my eyes over the words written on the page, I was appalled at what I saw. "This isn't my writing and my signature is forged. Premier Stalin, you need to see this. The ink has blotted up where the pen stopped before completing the letters on some of these words. Obviously, someone held the pen on the paper to copy the writing on another paper. I would never write this thickly. Give me a piece of paper and a pen and I'll demonstrate to you, to all of you exactly how I write and you will see it's nothing like this.

Beria turned to address the Party members. "Of course he would say something like this, but tell me something Marshal Zhukov, are you calling your comrade here a liar?"

"He's lying because you tortured him, you swine! Look at him!"

Beria lunged at me. "We told you what happened!"

"Do you expect me or any reasonable person to believe a story like that? If a robber comes into someone's house, he wants to get in and out. And if he really did get into a scuffle with my comrade here, why did he not kill him and killed his son instead?"

"Silence!" Stalin yelled. The room fell silent, but you could cut the tension with a knife. "I've heard enough! Send out the witness."

The officer grabbed my comrade by the arm, but he stopped to look at me. His eyes were filled with sorrow and you could see the guilt written all over his face. I looked at him with pity. I nodded at him to let him know it was alright and I didn't blame him. It was the truth; I never blamed him for what happened to me. He remained in prison for a few years until he wasn't needed anymore. When he got out, he was so consumed with guilt of what happened to me and his son's murder, he one day waited until his wife went out and hanged himself with a rope from the ceiling. Of course, this was covered up, and it was said that he had died from natural causes.

Back to that day, I watched my comrade walking towards the door like a weak and beaten down old man. My heart hurt thinking how else they could and would torture him.

"Marshal Zhukov," Stalin said. My attention immediately turned back up to him.

"After all this evidence that was presented here today, I find you guilty of treason and conspiracy to commit it."

I wasn't at all surprised by this. Stalin wanted me out of the way and Beria was all too pleased to help him accomplish this. I had to face the reality of that moment that I was going to be shot to death. "Premier Stalin, may I speak?"

"Make it short."

I looked around at all the members of the Party who were looking at me in disgrace. "I stand true to my word that I am not guilty of all this I am being accused of. The only thing I am guilty of is giving every fiber of my body fighting for my beloved country and the Party. I would never do anything to compromise your position in the eyes of the world, Premier Stalin. You can only properly serve your people by telling them the truth and fighting for it. That is all I have ever done for you. I hope you remember this as you sentence me."

Stalin sat in his chair, deep in thought. He gave me the once over and then stopped and looked at my medals. "Marshal Zhukov, you have served us all honorably, but that doesn't excuse what you have done." He took a deep breath and I matched this. I was nervously waiting for him to sentence me to death. The whole room was on edge in anticipation for Stalin to deliver his verdict. Beria was so excited; he was climbing out of his skin. "But in the end, it's your service and popularity with the people that has spared you. You will be condemned to the far outskirts of the country, far away from all of us. You are also banished from Party membership."

I let out a deep breath. For this I was relieved in the fact I wouldn't face the firing squad. Beria was shaking with anger.

He ran up to Stalin. "Premier, I beg you to reconsider. It's very dangerous to let him live. He can still correspond with his conspirators and he can still carry out his plot. You are going to have to always look over your shoulder." He was clearly trying to feed into Stalin's paranoia, making him so uncomfortable that he would change his mind and kill me.

"Enough!" Stalin yelled at the sniveling dog. "He will live in a place out of sight and out of mind where I can send my men to keep an eye on everything he is doing. Take him there now." The officer grabbed my arm and walked with me. The Party members stood up and shouted at me "traitor, traitor, traitor" until we walked out the door and their words were muffled mumblings.

Back inside, I learned what was discussed next from who was present in the room that day. Stalin had quieted everyone down. "Listen all! Marshal Zhukov is to be spoken of no more. He is dead to us! No one is to write of him. When the events of the war are written, his name will be written out and replaced with the names of others. In the future, let it be up to these so called historians to figure out what really happened."

Everyone in the room unanimously agreed. Stalin held true to his word of my fate. Years later, when people wrote of the events of the Great Patriotic War and discussed the many battles, my name was never mentioned, not even once. Things I had done and planned were given credit to people who were not even present or who were nothing more than merely an aide to Stalin at the time. It was as if I never even existed. All my blood, sweat, tears, and genius that I poured into preparations and carrying out the battles were erased by an author's pen.

What made matters even worse was the sharp contrast between my good friend Ike and me. Ike became President of the United States years later. I was so proud of him, and I admired the American people so much for wisely choosing a brilliant man and capable leader to represent them. People talked about his great accomplishments during the war and me, they might as well have written my obituary that day at my trial.

From the day after my trial on, I stayed in that small apartment. So many events occurred. I watched my oldest daughter get married and have children of her own. My youngest daughter was born and that was such a blessing to bring another child into the world. I was equally blessed to watch her grow into a beautiful, caring young woman. Unfortunately, my beloved wife passed away. I was forced to raise my little girl all by myself. While she was an absolute angel, a papa raising a child by himself is very difficult, especially a female child. She, however, grew up so fast and matured early enough to take care of herself.

Aside from my own family, I witnessed Ike's predictions come true. The Soviet Union and America became bitter enemies during our Cold War. The world didn't need the two super powers at bitter odds with one another. Wasn't the world emotionally drained from World War II, our Great Patriotic War? It was only a short time ago we all had witnessed mass murder and just how a human being could follow in the devil's ways. My biggest fear is that the memory of the horrors will fade away as people who lived through it grow older. Then to their children, the war is something that happened so long ago and they don't care to hear about it. This is so dangerous because those who don't learn from history are doomed to repeat its mistakes. One of my biggest motivations, besides restoring my good name, was to make sure people knew what happened and to prevent those horrible things from happening again.

Stalin's followers made this increasingly difficult. I always lived in great fear, on the edge of my seat that his officers would come to my door. They always arrived at my home in a pattern that would throw me off. They would show up on consecutive days and then they wouldn't show up for so long. So, I grew comfortable and let my guard down. Since I was essentially cut off from the world, the Cold War wasn't something I was dealing with. It was the Stalin vs. Zhukov war. I had to act like the old warrior I was in a different way. I had to outsmart him without using physical force. Two journals containing my memoirs had to be written- one that was false by praising Stalin's brilliance, and the other one that was true and is what you read now.

One night many years after my initial isolation, I was busily working on my true memoir. My health had been in decline for some time. I knew how important it was to finish this. Stalin's officers were after me, I could feel their tight grasp closing in on me. As I wrote furiously, I could feel their pursuit of me drawing closer. My heart beat faster as my pen whipped around the page, writing the words of truth.

SCCCRRRREEECCCHHHH! The sound of a car coming to an alarming halt caused me to look up outside the window. Even in the darkness, I could see by the street light that burned outside. There it was the black car that Stalin's secret police used to carry out their missions. The doors swung open and out came the three officers. Their dark blue uniforms shone brightly under the light. I jumped up from my chair and grabbed my journal off the desk. I attempted to run out the door of my office, but pains emanated from deep within my chest. I clutched at my chest in pain but still used all my strength to push myself forward. I darted down the short hallway and opened my little room in the corner. As I opened the door, I could hear the banging on the front door as the officers on the other side tried desperately to enter.

A groggy, young voice greeted me. "Papa, what's going on?"

I had awakened my precious little daughter Tatyanna. "It's ok, sweetheart. Please, go back to sleep." The hallway light lit up her room dimly, but I still found the floorboard near the wall in her room. I quickly threw off the dark green rug that covered the wooden floorboards in this part of her room. The banging grew louder on the front door as my fingers intricately worked to loosen up the floorboard. When it finally gave way, I placed the journal carefully inside and covered it with the black piece of cloth that lay inside. I placed the floorboard back, and replaced the dark green rug back in its place.

At this point, my chest pains grew more severe. I clutched helplessly at my chest and I responded with a loud painful groan that stirred my young daughter out of bed.

"Papa, what's wrong?" she asked worried as she crouched next to me on the floor.

Now, the front door gave way with a loud bang. "Marshal Zhukov," a deep, husky voice called out.

"Papa, who is that?" my little Tatyanna asked very frightened and unsure.

In spite of the tremendous pain in my chest, I jumped up. "Get back into bed and don't come out. No matter what you hear, do NOT come outside. Do you understand me?"

Her sad, questioning eyes hurt me. I knew I was potentially putting her in danger, but this was the only place I felt the journal would be safe and remain unsuspected to my pursuers. She walked back into her bed and crawled under the covers. I walked out the door and carefully shut it behind me. I could hear the officers rustling around in my office. I carefully walked down the hallway and stood in the doorway, watching them go through my desk and bookshelves. The one officer who was pulling out my drawers and going through the contents of them suddenly looked up when he appeared to see me from the corner of his eye.

"Where is it Marshal Zhukov?"

"Where is what?" I shot back in a passive-aggressive manner. I tried to appear calm and steady, but I still clutched my chest and breathed in deeply to try and relieve the pain as much as I could.

"The memoir you are working on. Stalin wants us to approve of the contents you have written."

I nodded my head in agreement and walked over to my bookshelf, past the two officers who were going through its books. I pulled out a journal with the two curiously watching me. I walked back over to the officer questioning me and looked him straight in the eye as I handed it over. He opened the journal and began to leaf through the pages, stopping every once in a while to concentrate on reading certain parts.

"Premier Stalin will be pleased with your praise of him."

I looked at him stone cold. "Good," I answered him. "I was getting ready for bed. Can I continue with what I was doing since you are obviously pleased with what I have written?"

The officer studied my face. His dark brown eyes cascaded gently over the wrinkles that reminded me of my age. He seemed to be searching for an answer to an unspoken question that he actively sought. His eyes seemed to grow more suspicious as he completed his study of my face. "I know you're hiding something! Keep searching men!"

"What are you doing? I showed you what you wanted!" I yelled out at them, trying to make my voice louder than the wild ransacking the three were carrying out.

They ripped apart my office like a furious storm releasing its powerful wind out and claiming the contents inside as its victims.

When the three officers were satisfied with their investigation of my office, they made their way into my kitchen to unleash their fury on it, searching for what would appease them. The one who had questioned me stopped and walked down the short hallway towards my daughter's room. I watched as my heart pounded out of fear of the journal being discovered, but even more importantly for worry over my daughter's safety. When he grabbed the door handle, it caused me to shout out. "That's my daughter's room! Please don't go in there. She's asleep."

He glared back at me, visibly angry that I interrupted his pursuit. He started to slowly twist the knob as we stared each other down. He finally opened the door and walked in. The pain in my chest grew more severe and I slowly sauntered down the hallway toward my daughter's room. I gripped at my chest as I stood in the doorway of my daughter's room. She was crouched in the corner of her bed with the covers pulled up to just under her eyes to conceal most of her face but she was still able to see what was happening. The officer stood in the middle of the room, actively looking around to see where he could continue his search next. My eyes affixed upon the dark green rug. As the officer searched around the room, my eyes never tore away from that rug. My chest pains grew more unbearable. It felt like sharp knives were digging deep into my chest.

Finally, the officer walked over to my daughter. She slouched down deeper under the covers. Her shaking vibrated the covers as they swayed along with her movement. "Did your papa hide something in here?"

Tatyanna just stayed under the covers and shook her head no.

My heart reacted to the sight of my daughter being dragged into the situation. Clutching my chest, I dropped to the floor and screamed out in pain. The officer walked over and stood above me.

He smiled watching me writhe in pain at the torture happening within my body. "We'll be back to check on you in the near future," he stated with no emotion. He walked out the door and all I heard was the sound of the front door closing.

My daughter jumped off her bed and crouched on the floor next to me.

From that point on, I was a shell of my former self. I spent my days in bed. When I could, I would sit up at my desk writing those truthful words in my journal. The officer kept his promise and did return to check on what I was doing. As if an act of God, he never discovered the exact hiding place of the journal.

However, it is yet to be determined if Stalin wins the fight and I continue to be written out of future historical records. It tortured me to have to actually praise him and write such garbage rather than completely focus on my true story that needed to come out. Whenever I felt the pain in my chest, I knew this was one battle of the war Stalin had won. I would fall to the ground, my chest in considerable pain. This was one of my numerous heart attacks that left me the shell of my former self.

This truthful journal is our final battle. I hope the people of the world know what I did and that my story will be passed from generation to generation. Whether I win the war against Stalin has yet to be determined. It is my hope that the Stalin head of the monster is finally slain by rewriting my presence of the war into books everywhere. To finish off, I would like to acknowledge my soldiers who fought under me. I hope you know how highly I think of all of you, and it was my great privilege to lead you into battle.

PRESENT DAY JUSTICE

I close my papa's journal, so emotional from what I had just read; tears were streaming down my face. How could I have forgotten that episode in my room all those years ago? I watched my papa suffer first hand, tortured by those officers with their dark blue uniforms.

What am I supposed to do next? I flip through the book, trying to find my papa's special instructions. There is a note attached to the back. "Tatyanna, go back to our apartment. My friend is waiting there to take this journal to a printer. Love, Papa.". It is attached to an enclosed envelope that is secured to the back of the journal. On the envelope, in my papa's handwriting it says, "The truth will always be revealed at some point in time". What is in this envelope? I thought to myself. Slowly and delicately, my fingers open the envelope so as not to disturb the writings on it.

When I open the flap of the envelope, a gold object catches my eye. The sun catches it at the right moment, and its gold aura is shining through to my eyes. Grabbing the crevices with my thumb and index fingers, I carefully pull it out and hold it up to examine it. When I see what is hanging on that necklace, my shock causes my breathing to pause momentarily. There it is- a

Star of David dangling gently in the air. My mind is completely empty of any thought except for one blaring one- did Hitler know that one of those he hunted became the hunter instead? A loud creak broke my concentration of this extraordinary realization. I put the necklace back in its envelope and carefully reseal it. Keeping the journal under the bed, I crawl out to investigate what is happening outside the door in the hallway. "Sasha?" I ask in a more subdued tone. I hear no answer. Walking down the hallway into the kitchen, I look around. "Sasha where are you?" Still I hear nothing.

Outside her front door, I hear the voices of men. I slowly walk up to the window and peer out from the corner. There they are my pursuers. It is funny how I am now no longer afraid of them. My papa's story has given me such inspiration and courage. To me now, they are just a blockade on my road to carrying out my papa's wishes. His story has to get out to the world and he left it in my hands to do it.

As they are trying to open the door, I dart back into Sasha's room. I look at the window and open it up to make it look like I had escaped out of it. I then dive under the bed.

"Spread out and find her!" One of the men's booming voices demand. The heavy footsteps boom through the hallway. I can hear opening and closing of doors. Until finally, the door of this room is flung open. I hold my breath so as not to be caught. The footsteps slowly come over near me. I watch as his feet stop by the bed. His feet shift and point at the bed.

"I know you're in here," he says. I, very carefully with the journal in my arms, slide across the floor under the bed to the side by the window with the hanging bedcover concealing my presence. Sure enough he looks under the side of the bedcover by the door. When I see him start to lift the cover up, I dart out from under the covers and start to dive out the window. Before I reach the window, the floor makes a creaking noise. The officer stands up and looks toward the window where he had heard the creaking noise, but I had already fallen outside He saw me going out of the window.

"She's escaping!" I hear him yell. I run as quickly as my legs will take me. I am still in pain from falling earlier, but I ignore it. I am determined to get back to my apartment. I keep turning around to see if they are gaining on me.

Running through the street, I hear a rumbling behind me. I turn to see a car heading straight for me. I don't need to see who is in the car to know who it is. The higher I pick up my legs, the faster the car comes toward me. I clutch the journal tightly to my chest. I hear the car within feet from me and in one last ditch effort I turn out of the way down an alley. Running down and out of the alley, I get back on the street leading to my apartment. Clutching the journal again, I pick up my legs. Turning around every once in a while to check for my pursuers, I am satisfied that I have lost them.

When I turn back around, a car has stopped in the middle of the road down ahead of me. I stop in place and try to catch my breath. The sweat is seeping through my clothes and I am drenched. The car and I are challenging the other to make the first move. Thoughts race through my mind of what I can do to lose them once and for all.

Finally, I figure out an ingenious plan. I run in the opposite direction. Immediately after I take my first strides, the car starts racing towards me. Faster and faster I run and there I see the wall of a building at the dead end of the street. That is my web of ensnarement for my pursuers. Breathing heavily as I get closer to the wall, the car comes dangerously close to me. I have to give every last bit of myself in this final attempt to get rid of them. If I am heading toward my death now, I want to know I have given it my all. Coming dangerously close to hitting the wall and with the car about to hit me, I throw myself out of the way. Then, there is blackness, nothing but blackness.

I wake up very groggy and with my head throbbing. Completely disoriented, I try to adjust and figure out what has happened. The light of the strong afternoon sun is hurting my eyes. I have to look through the slivers of my eyelids. Am I dead? Am I in heaven? Then a burning smell fills my nose. Have I gone to hell for not completing my task? I open my eyes more. Some feet away from me, the car that had been pursuing me is being eaten alive by the flames, caught in my wall trap. Finally, they are off my tail. I pick myself up with the journal and race along the streets back towards my apartment.

When I see the familiar structure I had lived in for so long, I smile as I run up my steps. I fling open the door to the welcoming sight of my furniture. I have never felt so happy to be home.

I hear footsteps from behind me and turn around. Sasha is standing there and smiles at me. I run over and give her a hug. "I'm so happy to see you," I said.

"I'm glad you're safe. Do you have the journal?"

I pull back in surprise. "Are you the one who's going to take it to the printer?

She nods her head to indicate that she is. I hand her the journal.

"No!" Someone shouts from behind me. I turn around to see a middle aged man with a gun. His hair is a grayish color and wrinkles can be seen through on his aging skin. He is pointing the gun at Sasha. Instead of being fearful, I am angry that he is threatening her.

"Who are you?" I shout at him.

"I need that journal," he says in a rather calm tone under the circumstances.

"You'll never get your hands on it!" I shout back at him.

"You don't understand. I made a promise to your papa years ago that I would help him by delivering that journal to a printer, Tatyanna."

I look at him, in shock. "How do you know my name?"

"I know all about you. Your papa was a very close friend of mine. I served under him during the war. My name is..."

"Vadim Petrov," I interrupted him.

He smiles at me. "You've heard of me." He is pleased that I know of him.

"Actually, I read of you in my papa's journal." I turn back over to Sasha, now confused. "Wait a minute. If my papa wanted Vadim to carry out his wishes, why are you here?"

"Because I'm the one he wanted," she answered.

"Liar!" Vadim yelled at her. "Tell her who you really are!"

"Taty, don't listen to him. It's me, your best friend. I want to help you and your papa."

"Tatyanna, listen to me. Her papa was a paid spy for Stalin. His assignment was to keep an eye on your papa. When he died, she took over the job for compensation. Her only job is to destroy that journal and keep the contents of it hidden forever."

My head is splitting and I feel so torn. Sasha is a sister to me. How can it be true what Vadim says? Then there is Vadim. I don't really know him. How can he turn against my papa? They were obviously very close. I look back and forth between the two, not knowing who to believe or trust. Sasha and Vadim continue eyeing each other and glancing at me every so often. "Give me back the journal, Sasha," I say.

She pulls away from me as I step toward her. "Come on, Taty. I can't do that."

Then, it occurs to me. If Vadim really is bad and wants to destroy the journal, he could easily have shot Sasha and myself and just taken the journal. "Sasha, I need you to give me the journal if you want me to believe you."

She looks at me and starts darting out the door when Vadim shoots the gun off. The bullet pierces her arm and she flinches, but still runs out the door. I begin following her, but Vadim interrupts me. "Wait!" I turn around. He runs up to me. "Take this. You're going to need it." I quickly grab the gun and run after Sasha.

She is so fast and keeping up with her is almost futile. However, my determination to get that journal propels my legs to pick up great speed. The race is exhausting and I ignore my broken toe. As I gain on her, she slowly pulls away. Exhaustion is overtaking Sasha, as she moves slower. I gain speed and start inching up close to her. Reaching out, I grab her hair and force her to the ground. She scratches my face with her nails. I am stunned from the pain and put my hand to my face to try and ease the pain. My anger swells up and POW- my fist finds its way into her right cheek. She still holds on tightly to the journal as I try to pry it from her arms. We are wrestling around, as I pull to get the journal free and she pulls it closer to her body. I can feel it coming loose. It comes closer and closer to me, until I feel her sharp teeth around my arm as the journal flies out of our grasp. She pushes me off of her to fetch the journal, but I grab her ankle and pull out the gun. I flip her on her back, so she is facing up. I hold the gun up to her forehead. "How could you do it? You were my best friend, my sister for heaven sake!" I shout at her.

"I did it for the rubles so I could survive," she answers looking deep into my eyes.

"You could deceive someone who was so nice to you?" She looks up at the gun. "You're not going to do it. You're too scared."

I slowly start to press the trigger. While looking at her, memories of our childhood fill me. Guilt comes over me, and I stop pressing the trigger. "Just let me give it to Vadim." She just looks at me, pushes me off, and grabs the journal. Without hesitation, I aim the gun and press the trigger. The bullet grazes her leg. Even though she was like my sister, she did commit the ultimate deception. She is standing in the way of my getting my papa's memoir out. I drop the gun, and it falls on the floor. Exhaustion sweeps over me due to the events of the day. Sasha remains on the ground with a grazed arm and a grazed leg. She is not moving. I grab the journal and hold it with all my might. Crying tears of joy that everything is over, but distraught over losing two people I love, is so surreal to me. Losing one of them to greed and deceit, is difficult enough, but losing my dear papa in the same day, is more than I can bear. As if nothing could save me, Vadim comes quickly over and takes the journal. He sees that I am alright and says, "I now take this journal to the printer."

EPILOGUE

My Cousin Killed Hitler helps assure that the shocking secret of World War II, held by my great-grandfather for over sixty years, is made known to the people of the world and not allowed to die with this author. The secret changes the look and feel of the entire War and holds in it what I feel is the greatest lesson in tolerance that the world has ever known. It became an obligation to write my book and the screenplay based on it, "Zhukov: Secrets of a World War II Hero," as I was the one to put the pieces together to reveal the secret. I was able to put the pieces together after being told a wealth of proprietary, disparate family information about this man who led directly to the kill of Hitler. My great-grandfather who is Marshal Zhukov's first cousin, carefully kept Zhukov's secret. He knew that if word got back to Stalin, and in later years to Kruschev, then his dear cousin Georgi would not have been allowed to rise up to the top position in the Soviet army. He also knew that Georgi would not have become the most decorated Marshal in the history of both the Soviet Union and present day Russia. Zhukov also could have been sent to prison if his secret were found out.

During the two years, I researched just about every publication ever written in any form about my fourth cousin, but nothing contained Zhukov's secret or any of my proprietary, family information. This propriety information spanned the time period from Zhukov's birth up through World War II. It was astounding to me that this was the case and I wondered how something so vital to history had not yet come out to the public in any way. Then I realized how my great-grandfather Isak, "Jak", a loving and dedicated family man, had carefully planned it to be this way. Jak died just about a year earlier than my cousin Marshal Zhukov and so even on his death bed, continued to protect him. Had it been the other way around, whereby my cousin had died first, I believe my great-grandfather would have revealed the secret.

To my amazement, I discovered from the facts reported in my research about my cousin, that Zhukov was the man most responsible for bringing an end to Hitler. I discovered that my cousin Zhukov and his men fought their way into Berlin to kill Hitler and drag his body through the streets of Moscow. Knowing this, Hitler was throwing a tantrum and said that if he would have had a general like Zhukov, he (Hitler) would have ruled the world. Hitler took poison and ordered his body be burned, knowing Zhukov wanted to get a hold of his dead body and drag it through the streets of Moscow.

I learned that my cousin was second in command of the Soviet Union during the World War II and that he had been in charge of fighting about eighty-eight percent of Hitler's army, while the Allies were fighting only about twelve percent of Hitler's army. I learned that Zhukov won more victories against Hitler than any other military figure. When I told my mother this, we both then looked at each other and coupled with our proprietary, family information said at the same time, "My God, we hold the greatest, shocking secret of World War II." It was then that I knew I had no choice but to let the world know the truth about my cousin Marshal Zhukov and World War II.

Again, my great-grandfather died in the early 1970's with the secret. My great-grandfather knew that if the secret got out about his cousin, then Zhukov would not have been able to use his genius to defeat Hitler. It was at a time when my great-grandfather's offspring were working hard to make their way in the world. As a result, time went by quickly and found the grandchildren in the 21st century, most all of whom had made lucrative and very successful careers. My mother was no exception and it was not until June 2008, that my mother told me about my cousin and all my great-grandfather's information about him. She only knew that my cousin was an important Marshal in the Soviet Army during World War II, what he was like as a child, and other detailed information about him throughout his life up through World War II, but did not know that he was the one most responsible for bringing down Hitler. My mother was the youngest and favorite grandchild, and as a very warm, sentimental, people-person, loved to hear all the family history and details that my great -grandfather would relate to her about my cousin, Georgi Zhukov.

My mother learned that Jak's male grandchild went in to the U.S. military in the early 1950s, as an officer after completing college and ROTC. This grandchild liked the army and wanted to make it his career. He applied to be accepted into the U.S. Military Counterintelligence at that time, but was denied because Counterintelligence, in their background search on him, had found out about this family relationship to Marshal Zhukov of the Soviet Union. My grandfather had never even told his grandson that he was related to Zhukov, so this came as a big surprise to this young officer. Therefore, our family relationship to my cousin Marshal Zhukov is contained in the governmental records of the U.S. Military Counterintelligence.

My Cousin Killed Hitler was written in a manner that requires the reader to pay close attention to every detail and to read the book carefully from cover to cover. I challenge the reader to discover the secret embedded in this book, just as I had to do in putting together the pieces of the puzzle to arrive at the secret. Zhukov had the genius at a young age to hide his true identity by changing his name and birth record in order to be conscripted into the army as a teenager. He was able to keep his secret from his wife and children, and although Stalin suspected his secret, he could never prove it. My book does just this. I hope it has been an amazing reading experience.

When I do get out for dinner or when running other errands, I am never free from this secret and never free from the burden of knowing that the vast majority of people walking about me do not know that they owe their freedom from Nazi rule to no one man more than to my cousin, as General Eisenhower said. If one looks on the internet's blogs and types in my cousin's name, there are a few around the world that do say that if it were not for him, the world would be ruled by Nazis and that mostly anyone who was not blonde and blue eyed would have already been exterminated. I have to agree with them. Also, I have great empathy with those whom I have met that have said when they were little, they remember the Nazi submarines right off their coast both in Florida and Long Island, New York. These people relay these stories and express their fear at that time, saying that they felt the Nazi's were just waiting to try and take over the United States as well.

Even though I know my cousin as the man that he truly was from the information passed down to me from my great-grandfather, as I said, I learned from my readings of the facts of how truly great and what a military genius he was. I highly respect

General Dwight D. Eisenhower and have to listen again, to what General Eisenhower said when he spoke in Frankfurt in June 1945: "In Europe the war has been won and to no one man do the United Nations owe a greater debt than to Marshal Zhukov" (for the defeat of Nazi Fascism and the termination of the Holocaust). My Cousin Zhukov's successes go on and on. He was an honest and straightforward man who did not discriminate against anyone based on their race, color, religion, or creed. Because of this, there were Generals under him who rose up in the ranks who otherwise would not have been able to. His cousin Jak and he shared many qualities including these just mentioned.

In the year of 1941, the Germans invaded the Soviet Union with passionate and unyielding force. The Soviets were unprepared and powerless to stop the enemy. In response to this invasion, the Soviet government had established partisan units that engaged in guerilla warfare against the German invaders. The Soviets had to resort to animalistic instincts in order to help equalize the battlefield. In the ghettos in Minsk and Belorussia, the Jews inside were being treated like animals and denied their basic rights and dignity that human beings enjoy. My cousin Marshal Zhukov was assigned to form a partisan unit and help to oversee it. What he did with this assignment is a testament to the kind of person he was and how strongly he secretly felt about his faith. He arranged for the Jews to escape from these ghettos and join his partisan unit, ignoring the requirement that they come with weapons of their own. Marshal Zhukov arranged for weapons to be issued to them so they could fight against the enemy, and carry on in helping other Jews escape from ghettos. Hundreds of Jewish lives were saved because of Marshal Zhukov's partisan unit. Many Jews who survived the war and evaded imprisonment in concentration camps have attributed this to serving under Marshal Zhukov's command in the Red Army.

Most people in modern times do not realize how strong anti-Semitism was in the Soviet Union. Marshal Zhukov grew up hearing stories of how the Cossacks came into the Jewish villages and killed his Aunt and Uncle by beating them with a broken leg of a chair. From a young age, he knew he wanted to serve in the Soviet army and accomplish great things. However, he was also aware that being Jewish would limit him in this quest for greatness. Zhukov rose to the highest rank in the Soviet army, as he was successful in hiding that he was Jewish. There were Jews who held positions of power in the army, but I firmly believe that this was attributed to my cousin wanting to help his fellow Jews.

Millions of Jews lost their lives during World War II because they held on to their faith that was loathed by a madman. Marshal Zhukov held his faith close to his heart and made a difficult decision to hide it. This was not a cowardly act, but a very intelligent one. Imagine if he had not done this? Who else would have stood up to Stalin and forced him to listen to his brilliant strategy without fear of the firing squad for defying the Premier? The Jews needed one of their own to be in a position of power to defeat Hitler. It's only a shame that Hitler did not know that one of those he hunted became the hunter instead.

Cousin Georgi had no choice but to be ruthless and stern as he knew he was not only fighting for the survival of his own family, but for the survival of his beloved Soviet Union and the rest of the world. He was an empathetic person who felt deeply for all his soldiers, and subsequently dedicated his memoirs to them.

When I relay to students about my cousin through the contents of this book and tell them that I am the cousin of the man who did all I have already mentioned, they become enthralled and somehow history comes alive for them. This experience for them, I feel, will be one step in helping assure that my cousin's legacy is not lost to time, and that his great secret will serve to become the premise for one of the greatest lessons in tolerance for our present and future generations. We must learn from the lessons of the past or be destined to repeat the mistakes. I hope this book restores my cousin to his rightful place in history.

ABOUT THE AUTHOR

The author, Hera Jaclyn Becker, was born on February 1, 1985 and raised in South Florida where she currently resides. She is an author, and screenplay writer. Her script entitled: <u>Zhukov: Secrets of a World War II Hero</u>, which was based on *My Cousin Killed Hitler,* has received praise from agents and producers in Hollywood, California.

Hera Becker earned her M.B.A at 21 years of age from the H. Wayne Huizenga School of Business and Entrepreneurship at Nova Southeastern University. This makes her one of the youngest recipients of an M .B A. While attending graduate school, she was engaged in another very admirable, philanthropic endeavor. Hera developed trademarked, greeting cards and a concomitant card company that is the only card company specifically for non-traditional families.

Hera's research found that seventy-two percent of families in this country are non-traditional families in that they do not have both a natural mother and natural father. She did this in her empathy for the children of 9/11 who lost parents in the attack. She wanted these children to have their own line of cards that would help them express their appreciation to their new caregivers. Since then, an organization of 9/11 families included as part of their website a section for those caregivers who have taken over for many of the parents lost in the attack.

In addition, Hera's greeting cards were recognized by the Florida Education Association (FEA), the National Education Association (NEA,) and the Nova Southeastern University newsletter, Sharkbytes. The FEA featured a two page article about the greeting cards and their benefit to children as well as the fact that for every card purchased, a significant portion of the proceeds would go to the largest non-profit children's charity in the world.

The author was very touched by this quote. "History is always written wrong, and so always needs to be rewritten." This was stated by the great philosopher George Santayana. It is not so much that history was written incorrectly, but it is that much is left out and lost to family knowledge that never gets passed down to the younger generations. Thank goodness, in the history surrounding her fourth cousin Marshall Georgi Zhukov, the true history of World War II will not be lost to family knowledge that was never clearly and connectedly passed on to the younger generation. It was just by chance, that this author, put two and two together to combine disparate pieces of family information together to reveal, what many people will surely feel, is the greatest, shocking secret of World War II. This secret has been held in her family's knowledge for sixty years since the beginning or World War II. Once the author pieced this together and realized that she alone held this great secret, she became obligated to publish this book so this would not be lost forever and the people of the world would come to know the secret themselves. The secret is vital in that is it changes the aura and total view of World War II. The author is a very compassionate and empathetic person as attested to by these endeavors, and if not for all these separate pieces of knowledge and personality traits, this secret would have died with the author's family. This would have been a great loss to the world. The prophetic statement by Krishna Menon, the 1957 Ambassador from India in Moscow, is coming true through the publication of *My Cousin Killed Hitler*. He said, "The Party (Stalin and the Communist Party) may succeed in keeping Zhukov's figure out of the public eye, but it will not succeed in keeping his memory out of the hearts of men."

The author felt that her cousin Marshal Georgi Zhukov was denied his clearly deserving place in the history of all countries. She set out to see that this underdog got his rightful place and that the people of the world learned about this man to whom they are most indebted to for their current way of life that is free from the tyranny of Hitler.

Please visit the author's website at
http://www.happyfatheringday.com

Printed in the United States
by Baker & Taylor Publisher Services